Lithium*buzz*

by

Andrew P. H. Clyde

authorHOUSE®

AuthorHouse™
1663 Liberty Drive, Suite 200
Bloomington, IN 47403
www.authorhouse.com
Phone: 1-800-839-8640

First published by AuthorHouse 5/27/2008

ISBN: 978-1-4343-8870-4 (sc)

Printed in the United States of America
Bloomington, Indiana

This book is printed on acid-free paper.

Author's Note

According to the National Institute of Mental Health, over 26 percent of the U.S. population suffers from mental illness. This covers everything from manic-depression/bipolar disorder, obsessive-compulsive disorder, schizophrenia, schizo-affective disorder, or any other ailment that cripples the mind. That percentage means that nearly 57 million people living in the United States are suffering from an illness that some think is merely a matter of "overcoming" something that is all mental. Mind over matter—only the strong survive.

I'm here to tell you that mental illness can't be turned off like a light switch. It's something that millions of people have to live with, as some people have to live with cancer, multiple sclerosis, heart disease, or chronic halitosis. There is no difference, whatsoever, between the terminal illness of people suffering from cancer and people suffering from schizophrenia. More than 90 percent of suicides in this country are committed by people suffering from a mental disorder. Death is as much a risk for someone suffering from manic-depression or schizophrenia as it is for someone who's been diagnosed with cancer. Céline, in *Journey to the End of the Night* (1936), wrote, "The truth of this world is death." In other words, life is death. And death is death. And what makes one death less tragic than another? If one dies a slow and agonizing death as cancer eats away at his lungs, or if one kills herself because she cannot live with voices corrupting her brain, whispering in her ear, or her mind telling her that her thoughts are being intruded on by unknown entities, which death is worse?

Death is tragic in any form, and to make the claim that one death is worse than the other, you just have to wonder, if this man's lung cancer was brought on by thirty years of smoking, what caused this woman's schizophrenia? God? Her environment? Whatever the reason, he wanted to smoke and she didn't want schizophrenia. Yes, cancer is a terrible thing, and no one asks for a disease. What I am trying to dissuade people of is the notion that mental illness is not as big a problem, or as horrible a torture, as cancer or MS or any other disease out there that wrecks lives and kills horribly.

Just as there are differing symptoms of a physical disease, there are varying symptoms of mental disease as well. Some schizophrenics are able bodied and can function in society with proper medication. When off their medication, they can hear voices and hallucinate, but are otherwise functional members of society. However, this is not always the case. Some schizophrenics suffer from more paranoia than others. Some hallucinate more than others, who hear more voices than those of the ones standing next to them. People suffering from bipolar disorder (manic-depression) can sometimes go from completely manic to cripplingly depressed in a matter of sometimes less than an hour. Others are primarily manic, while others still tend to veer more towards depression. Obsessive-compulsives are sometimes severely disabled; others simply seem "quirky" like the character in the television show *Monk*.

Personally, I suffer from schizo-affective disorder, the disorder Marcus Dolby suffers from in the novel you are about to read. My own symptoms include paranoia, auditory hallucinations, obsessive-compulsive symptoms, visual hallucinations, mania, depression, and what a psychiatrist I saw while living in New York City called "cyclical thinking." What this means is that a traumatic event, in some cases the use of a narcotic, or seeing someone get shot and killed in the street, can be a trigger for this symptom. When this happens, the mind—my mind, at least—goes in circles. I will think thoughts both delusional and paranoid, some simple thoughts like "I need to use the bathroom," but each thought leads into the other, one thought forming a new one, going in a circle until returning to the original one, which in my case, usually has to do with my own death. It is almost like a panic attack, but much more severe.

Marcus Dolby's symptoms in *Lithiumbuzz* are very similar to my own symptoms. In fact, there are some incidents in this story that actually happened to me, personally, and to my family. The character of Donald, Dolby's brother, can symbolize the ideals of any family dealing with someone with severe mental illness, a person who has been in and out of mental hospitals and whose life is something less than perfect. Families tend to blame themselves for the sickness of the mentally ill member. They often go to great lengths to make the ill family member well again. But most importantly, they simply want the pain of the mentally ill brother or sister or mother or father or cousin or uncle or aunt or whoever to end. They want the person to be happy and normal. And when that doesn't happen—or can't happen—they, themselves, become sick with agony at having to watch their loved one delve deeper into their illness and become worse and worse.

So those who still believe that mental illness is relegated to people running in circles, covered in their own filth, talking about the end of the world on the streets of New York, need to remember that even those people have families, and even they were children once. And even they can find help. The goal of this novel is to shed some light on who these people are. Marcus Dolby is a man who had a normal existence: he had a job, a girlfriend, a loving family. But his mental illness simply got in the way. I have always insisted that I am not my disease; that my disease is a part of who I am, but it is not *who* I am. I am a person with a wife, a family, and a job. But when I get sick, I am no different from the man babbling in the street professing how he is the reincarnation of Jesus Christ. There is help for all people with mental illness. The problem is that some people simply don't care, or wish to sweep the problem under the rug. Out of sight, out of mind. They don't want to be bothered. It makes them uncomfortable to even be near someone with mental illness.

We are people, just like you. Just like your uncle who had cancer. Just like your mother who suffered from rheumatoid arthritis. There is no us; there is no them; there is only *we*: we the afflicted, we the men and women who live each day with disease and illness. All I ask is that at the end of reading this book, you think about someone you know who you feel is just a bit odd, or off, or overly emotional, or weird, or just plain nutty, and realize that he or she is a person, too. He or she has real feelings and real pains; they have dreams of a better life, just as you do. All I ask is that you look at yourself not as someone who is better than he or she is, but as someone who can make a real difference in their lives. You can change them. You cannot make them better: nothing cures crazy. But you can be a savior to them. Talk to them, listen to them, but above all, be there *for* them. Because all he or she wants is for someone to listen to them, just as I want you to read this and listen to me.

It's true; the truth of the world *is* death. But the other truth is that life is the world's great commonality. What I want from you is to look at your life and look at the life of someone you know, or someone you see who is mentally ill, and realize that when it all comes down to it, that is our common bond. No matter how different or weird or crazy someone may seem, you, them, we all share life. And a life together is far more enjoyable than a life of seclusion for *them,* and a life of fear and confusion for *the others.*

We're all in this together.

I think I speak for 57 million people when I say, "Just listen to us. That's all we ask. We just want our voices to be heard."

So listen.

Please.

—Andrew P. H. Clyde

May 1, 2008

The Author's Thanks to...

I want to thank many, many people, some of whom I won't be able to name here due to space. First and foremost, I want to give my thanks and my undying love to my wife, Demetria. She has been my rock and my life since the day we met. She never let me quit even when I wanted to. I love you so much boo. L. Heartfelt thanks to my family, my brothers Tom and John—the real life "Donald"—who have always made sure my insanity didn't ruin me. I love you both. Loving and sincere thanks to mom and dad, two people who have loved me unconditionally and supported my wife and me through the lean times. Without them, we would not survive. Gary and Lois, I mean this with my whole heart: I love you both. Cathy and Elwood, I wouldn't have gotten through this without you. Much love. Dame, Rob and Marilyn, thank you from the depths of my soul.

A special thinks to Andrea Talarico of Anthology Books in Scranton, PA. Before she owned her own bookstore she helped me get through *Lithiumbuzz* by giving advice, free editing, critiques, creative sound boarding and was a huge supporter of me and my work throughout the writing process. I literally could not have done this without you. (No matter what you say to the contrary!) Other thanks go to Kevin Lewis who gave me the intro to the book. To Dan DeJoseph who has been a dear friend to me, and never let my illness get in the way of our friendship. To my Wilkes University creative writing master's program classmates who have always inspired me to keep going. To Dr. Bonnie Culver who never let me give up. To Mister Jim (Warner), a man who has always been good to me and said, "You *are* a good writer, Andrew." To Nina Solomon, who never let me forget that talent is not something learned, and never let me forget that I did, indeed, have some. (Whether I believe it or not.) To David Poyer who let me know what needs work in my writing, and showed me that I still have a lot to learn; and to Lenore Hart, all three of these great writers have been my guides for the past year.

And to the people at AuthorHouse. Thanks to Melanie Loehwing, my editor, Vid Beldavs for his support, Margaret Turner, Rita Dawson, Trina Lee, and each and every one of those who helped me get this published. It would be impossible to name every person who got me going on my career, but a special thanks to everyone one of you.

Many thanks to all of you, and to any I may have forgotten.

Dedication

To Demetria: my friend, my wife, the love of my life.

L

"My name is Legion; for we are many."
New Testament: Mark 5:9

ONE: *The House of Cheese*

… I guess my last real, lucid, vivid memory was of my widowed mother crying—weeping—as she watched my roommate Bailey take a shit on the floor in the mental ward of St. Michael the Hope …

Wait.

The knife seems to glide across my skin. Nothing. It would be nice to feel something. *Anything!* I feel the blood dribble down my neck, the evil wetness of it seeping into my shirt collar. My mind bubbles to life with the realization that I'm about to die! This is it! I cut deeper! Deeper! Yes! I'm gonna die! Wait, wait, wait, wait, wait, wait …

I'm in my living room and I get a call from Marianne, my girlfriend, and she tells me that something just ran into her building. (Some asshole flew a fucking plane into her building downtown.) Later I turn on channel four. Horror. I watch the tape as another jet runs into the other tower, and about an hour or two later, they both fall over with her and thousands of other people inside as well.

Wait.

Memories, memories, memories. *Sometimes memories keep you sane*, says Donald.

Memories of my existence caught in the creases of my brain: Mother holding, Father leaving, teacher yelling, everything just a memory. Memory with a capital *M*. So, so, so, what do I recall? What do I know is real? Tell me tell me tell me, because I have to know! You've got to do this, just once! Write them, shout them, think them, but dear God, hurry! Dear God, make it quick because there's not much time now!

No! Please no!

I guess my last memory was—

Wait, wait, wait …

My last memory was—

No, no … wait.

Okay. Calm. Relaxed. Think now.

Now try try try!

Do it!

***

Mother's hand firmly, firmly holding mine as we walk the length of the asphalt leading up to the tank where the penguins wait, black feathered backs drooping like melted wax as they plummet off the rocks and into the coldcold water, splishsplashing filthy, blue water over the side of the tank, and that's all it is, a tank: *These birds should fly away*, I think to myself as Mother holds my hand as we hike past the tank now and over to the pit where the polar bears munch noisily on some fish. And I realize that I'm too old to be holding hands with Mother …

No.

Wait.

There is something else.

Yesyes.

The car, stifling hot—can barely breath as Mother closes the door, trapping me and Donald and Suzie inside the Dasher—Volkswagen's finest diesel, no doubt—the door's shut with us three inside gasping for air, but all's well that ends well, as we're going to the zoo to watch the animals frolic and play and eat other animals, which I love! And it's okay to not breathe as long as there's a zoo to go to.

Yes?

No. Wait, there's more to this than that.

Wait.

Yes, now I—yes!

The eggs sit on the plate in front of me like two eyes waiting to be slashed, yolk oozing out like plasma from stone, thenthenthen Mother walks over with the toast, and then the potatoes—fried potatoes, yes!—and then I eat, or do I? Yes! I eat it all and this is good because I never eat all my food, especially in the morning, as who has an appetite at seven o'clock—not me, never do. If I eat all my food I get to have licorice in the car on the way to the zoo, where we will watch bears and birds and lions and leopards.

Yes!

So that trip to the zoo with me and Donald and Mother and Dad—Suzie wasn't dead yet, and we—all of us, yes!—are in the car, the hothot car, driving past the buildings of downtown—looks like rain as I stare listlessly at the sky—and as we get to the parking lot of the zoo, Mom stops the car and puts the licorice in her purse, we get out, yesyesyes! Now I know!

We get out of the car and Mom grabs my hand. She seems sad, or angry, or sleepy—can't tell which—and we walk.

Yes! Now I—

There are all kinds of trouble when my sister gets lost in the spider house after showing me the tarantulas with their spiny fangs and bristles for hair, and the legs that tepidly feel around for something firm to walk on. And she's gone. And this is different, this has never happened before, not this, nono, not like this, because Mom never feels this way when one of us wanders off; there's always a sense of certainty that we're right around the corner—my brother or sister or me—right there, just beyond the eye line; maybe bending over to tie a shoelace, or pick up gum still safe within the five-second rule. No, this is different, and when she's not there an hour later, or two, or three, and when she's not there after a night and a day, then, then Mother starts shouting at my father that he never pays any goddamn attention to us kids and *What the hell is wrong with you anyway?* she spits.

But they do find her four days later in Ronny Feldham's garage on Bachman Avenue. She was scared and crying, but not hurt—thank God—but she didn't talk for a while after that, and when she did talk, she cried. Then she stopped talking again. Then, later, she died.

But that's what I can recall. Mother's hand firmly, firmly holding mine as we walk the length of the asphalt leading up to the tank where the penguins wait ...

***

Suzie sits at home and sews a blood red heart and a shit brown cross into embroidery cloth as Dad reads a mystery book. Mom is in the kitchen glancing out the window at Donald, my brother, as he throws a tennis ball against the garage—still painted blue, not white like after Suzie died—catching it in his old baseball mitt. Mom watches him, and she doesn't hear Suzie muttering mutteringmuttering nothings under her breath. No one hears her, not Mom, not Dad, certainly not Donald, but I do. I do because I'm sitting right behind her on the sofa as she does cross-stitch, and I hear her words, and—Yes! Yes! Yes!—I hear what she says and when I tell Mother later, when I tell her what Suzie said, she slaps my face and scolds me. Then she starts to cry and she holds me and says, *I'm sorry, baby! I'm so sorry!* but I'm not certain she's even talking to me anymore. Just crying and rocking me as she weeps, me feeling her snot on my shoulder, her tears on my arm. I feel uncomfortable, and I tell Mom I can't breathe, and that reminds me of that day, the day in the car going to the zoo.

And I remember distinctly walking with my hand in Mother's, walking the length of the asphalt, walking to the penguins, and feeling the water splishsplash against my naked legs as we pass.

***

Ronny Feldham's house was brick and stucco, looked like muenster and cottage cheese. Every time we passed it before we lost Suzie I got hungry for cheese—any cheese, nothing in particular. And then we lost Suzie and found her in the house of cheese, and after that I always thought of that one day in the living room, three weeks after finding her in the garage. Every time we passed the house from then on I thought of her mutteringmuttering nothings under her breath. Now I'm never hungry for cheese. Muenster or otherwise. And when we pass the house I don't even think of cheese. Instead I think of that day, the day of Mother crying and her snot on my arm. I think of Suzie muttering. Nothings. Under her breath.

Stick me with that and I'll bite it off! (she hisses) *Do it again and I really bite it off this time!* (she hisses)

When I tell mother later what Suzie said, she slaps me and scolds me and cries and sends me to bed.

***

The summer we painted the house and the garage white was our first summer as a family of cold, bitter, angry people. With Suzie laid in the dirty ground— worms and bugs and stones—we all did our parts. I did the garage with Mother. Dad did the house with Donald. Mother didn't want to do the house with Dad, she told me in secret—*Don't tell your father,* she whispered. *Don't say anything,* she said.

When we've finished the garage, Mom tells Dad that she's done enough painting for one lifetime and needs a break. Dad rolls his eyes. Mom yells at him. Dad shakes his head. Mom shouts. Dad sighs. Then Mother leaves and goes away, and doesn't come back for some time. Dad starts smelling bad, like cough syrup tastes, like hairspray smells. When Dad is home, he takes long pulls from a bottle and falls asleep watching baseball every night until the World Series starts. Then Mom comes back. She tells him she's home. He's too tired to say anything, so he turns over and falls asleep again.

Mom goes to the door and whispers something to a man dressed in brown tweed; the man kisses Mom and I feel angry, not because he's kissing Mom, but because she's kissing him back. And all the while, Dad is sleeping right across the hallway in the living room where the Mets just won the Pennant.

After the World Series, Dad leaves the house every night at six thirty and comes back at eight. He doesn't smell like anything but coffee now.

When Dad is out after dinner until eight, Mom's friend comes over—the man wearing the brown tweed also wears houndstooth, pinstripes, corduroys, argyle sweaters, all of them smelling like cigars. Mom doesn't seem to mind the smell, but she does yell at me when I find them without their clothes on and Mom scolds me and closes the door. Then the man leaves after swearing at me, and Mom tells me that *It's going to be our little secret*, she says. *Don't tell your father*, she says.

***

And I sit in my room as winter begins, with my bed next to the radiator, and it's so hot that I can barely breathe. And I remember, suddenly, as I lay there trying to doze off, that day in the car, the hothot car—the Dasher—and I remember munching on a rope of licorice, sharing it with Suzie, the both of us eating, talking about birds and bears and lions and whatall.

***

Mom holding my hand as we make our way past the penguins—

Suzie right behind us with Dad—

Donald wandering in front of Mom, waiting for a second or two, then walking ahead some more.

Then the spider house. And Suzie shows me a tarantula as she's touching my shoulder and pointing. She's telling me about the tarantula. Then I start to ask a question, something like, *When tarantulas die, what heaven do they go to ...?* But she doesn't answer me, and I realize that her hand isn't on my shoulder.

I turn and see everyone but my sister. I ask Mom where Suzie went. Mom says she must have gone ahead. But she didn't. No. No she didn't. She's in Ronny Feldham's garage. That's where she is.

Then we found her.

Then she did cross-stitch.

***

I found her body in the basement of our blue house on Walnut Street. I screamed but nothing came out. I screamed and screamed but nothing but air came out. She wouldn't wake up. Even when I shook her, she wouldn't wake up. I tried to scream but nothing came out. I screamed and screamed and screamed, but all that came out was air and a whispery squeal. And she wouldn't wake up, even though I tried tried tried to wake her. But she wouldn't.

That's what I remember.

***

Sitting in class as teacher reads the report—the paper on Martin Luther, the Lutheran, not the leader—the class is giddy with anticipation: What will the freaky freak write? Will it be swears, or will it be gibberish? The freak—Me, Me with a capital *M*—sits alone in the back and waits for the laughter to begin as teacherteacher reads what I wrote. He reads what the freak wrote, which is, mainly, drivel: drivel about a man who lived 500 years ago and started Lutheranism. The paper is concluded with a thesis that includes the fact that Mr. Luther was something of an egomaniac, naming an entire religion after himself. *What?* (the paper goes) *Does Martin Luther dare to attempt being Christ by naming a religion after himself?* (the paper goes) *And to think that Jesus wrote that the first shall be last. There is a dark, warm place in hell for Martin Luther ...*

Yes!

Teacher stops reading, stands there, slack jawed at the audacity of this walking freak show, this boy who dares to blaspheme the name of the holiest man in all of Lutherandom. The Jesus Christ of Lutheranism. The German Christman who saved men's souls and gave the world fucking Lutherans, the very men and women who run the fucking Lutheran school he sits in at this very moment in time. If Luther hadn't invented Lutheranism, there'd be no fucking Lutheran school in this town, and this tub 'o freak would be a goddamn illiterate.

Teacher smiles deviously and looks at the freak and says rather plainly, *You'd better hope he puts in a good word for your sister, Mr. Dolby ...*

It's been five years, and—

Yes—wait—yes!

The air conditioner in the ceiling, blowing in dirty, crusty air from the other rooms, blowing right onto my head. No one cares that the air is blowing right on my head, because I'm not a fucking Lutheran. I'm a goddamn

Catholic. There are no Catholic schools in town. Thus, I'm sent here. Christian schools are fun!

Teacher blasphemes the memory of my sister, Suzie. Suzanne. The girl who was found in Feldham's garage. (No tears. Please God, no tears.) I stare in anguish. Teacher stands in the front of the room, smiling at me.

No! Stop! Don't cry.

I want to run, and I want to never come back to this fucking Lutheran school again—St. Martin's Lutheran School. I wait for him to stop smiling, his Cheshire grin a mask of the evil just behind those nicotine-stained teeth. I keep waiting, but he won't stop smiling.

Even my thirteen-year-old head knows he's mind-fucking me.

***

GagGagGag, it all comes up …

I try in vain not to vomit as the beer swirls around my mouth and splishsplashes in my stomach. I feel the vomit inching up my esophagus; I gag, and there's nothing I can do, only hide my head from my friends so they won't see the puke gushing from my mouth.

What's with you, Dolby?

Fuck, man! Are you puking?

I knew this was a fucking mistake, letting Freakshow tag along.

My only three friends in the whole world, Mike and Pat and Keith, sit in a circle drinking. I am on the outside of the circle. These are my friends who aren't my friends.

You have the smokes, Dolby? At least tell me you brought the smokes, Mike says.

I pull out the cigarettes I stole from Goldberg's Supermarket. They all take a pack and open them and light up. They inhale. They exhale. Then they ignore me for the rest of the night.

***

I'm on a date with Mary Ann.

Mary Ann is a sweet girl with a tilted smile and pert nose and doughy breasts that I've never felt, but always wanted to. Always wanted to feel them and I dream of them.

Wait! Yes, that's one!

Mary Ann! Think of Mary Ann!

I dream of Mary Ann at night when I'm alone, touching myself sometimes. I think of her lips and eyes and nose—nothing dirty, no, not Mary Ann. She's clean and no one can make her dirty, not even my perverted mind.

I wish she'd look at me more. I wish she'd follow me around the way I follow her around. I wish she'd wish I'd look at her more. The more I think of her, the more my stomach hurts, the more I sweat, the more I stink. I look at her and my mind hurts, too. She's the only one who doesn't laugh at me.

She's the only one who makes me feel human.

I wish I wish I wish …

***

I'm in the ward now. I'm alone. Mom is supposed to come and see me this afternoon. I tried to tell her that I don't want visitors. She never listens. For my own good. No one listens to me.

I wait now in the day room, playing cards with a girl named Donna, whom I have decided to have a crush on; no matter that she's loonier than I am. No matter that her wrists are sliced open. She shows me the gash right underneath her palms; the stitches stick out of her skin like cacti. Little cactus needles sticking out of her wrists. I took pills. Everyone in the ward says I'm a faggot for taking pills. That only fags take fucking pills, and *You must be a fag because you tried OD-ing on fucking pills. Fucking Bayer, no less. You must be some stupid faggot, thinking you can OD on Bayer.*

Fuck you fuck you fuck you!

Forget that! No, don't let that be one of them! Forget the whole—

Mom comes and says that I look terrible, *Terrible, just look at you! You're a disaster! My stars, I raised a slob …*

How's Dexter, Mom?

He's fine, thanks.

How's Dad?

He's fine, too.

Dexter is the man in the tweed and argyle and houndstooth and whatall. They kissed in the doorway when Dad was sleeping while the Mets were dousing themselves with Korbel.

It's Suzie's anniversary ...

Yes, says mother. Suzie. Right.

She never existed; my mother has rubbed her out. No licorice, no zoo, nothing. Suzanne never was. Not to Mother, at any rate.

How's Donald?

He's fine.

Where is Donald?

He's at home.

Why didn't he come?

No answer. I wish he was here. I wish I could make him feel better. I wish I wish I wish.

He's going through this, too, you know.

Whatever, Mom.

The orderly knocks on the door. It's time for Mom to go. I didn't want her to come, but I don't want her to go now. I need her to stay. Don't go, Mother! But she has to, and I don't want that. I don't want her to go, because then I'll be alone with the mean bastards and Slashy McGee and her Magic Wrists. I don't want to play cards any more! I want to go home and watch TV or read or do something, anything! Anything but sit here in this fucking ward and wait for my sanity to kick in!

No! Jesus Christ, no.

Wait! Wait! Wait!

I know!

It's graduation night and I'm with Marianne, and the friends who aren't my friends are there, but they don't like me, and Marianne and I are at this party, and it's just me and Marianne—who tells me that she's going away, to London (or was it Glasgow?), and she just wanted to tell me because she wants me to be the first to know. That she was accepted at such and such university, that she was going to go at the end of the summer. And wouldn't it be great if I could come visit her there in Glasgow? (Or was it London?)

***

I'm at my desk at Daniels & Webster Publishing, and Mr. Deets is glaring at me, showing his pearly teeth, his eyes like fire pokers, hot and red, pokepokepoke, they jab and gouge me. After the last one—the last time I went nuts—he threatened to fire my ass—*I'm going to fire your ass,* he said. *I'll find something on you. Just give me an excuse!*

The next day I come into the office and find everyone staring at me. The day after the freak-out I walk in and all eyes are on me. What happened, see, is that my mind went. It does that now and then, and it went.

You're a fuck-up, Dolby! Deets says.

Sorry, sir, I say.

Look at this proposal; you okay'd it without consulting your team. That's what a team is for, goddamn it! he says.

I'm sorry ... (Mind going now, stand back, everyone.)

We already put in about twenty grand on this hack and you sit there and tell me you're sorry. Well, fuck your apology! That money ought to come right out of your paycheck.

Sorry, I'm really so—

You say sorry *once more and I'll kick your fucking ass!*

Yes, sir ... (What? Do what? Do what to him?)

You cocky little shit! With your fucking—

Thenthenthen I stand and I scream at the top of my lungs, I scream, *You cocksucking shit! You fucking prick, you don't fucking talk to me*—(I'm screaming)—*like that! I'm not a fucking child! You fuck! I'll fucking kill you!*

I go to my desk hearing gasps. Spazz. Freak. Etc.

The air around the office is dense with confusion and fear and incomprehension. No one here will ever know what it's like to lose control. No one here knows what it's like to be afraid of yourself. No one here understands my fear and madness.

Next day, I'm afraid as I step off the elevator and into the office, with all eyes glued to me. I'm at my desk at Daniels & Webster Publishing, and Mr. Deets is glaring at me, showing his pearly teeth, his eyes like fire pokers, hot and red, pokepokepoke, they jab and gouge me.

And this is me, and this is where it starts. Maybe not here exactly, but for all intents and purposes ...

Wait.

TWO: *Half Asleep in a Gravel Pit*

Get away!

Run and hide!

Save yourself and save your children; don't let them get too close; I may bite and infect you with my sickness. I might give you crazy. Runrunrun! I might be contagious. Get away, now now now now now, gogogogogo! Get gone and hurry doing it, because I'm dangerous; ask anyone who knows nothing at all about what I'm talking about.

It's all mental …

Rise above …

The only medication you need is a positive attitude …

Yeah, *I'm* sick. Ask anyone. They'll tell you; but don't ask me. No no! Steer clear, make way, *Unclean, unclean!* God *damn* it I wish someone would listen to me! I wish I wish I wish someone, *anyone*, could understand me, know me, fix me! But the only reaction is fear; the only consolation is nervous or embarrassed laughter; the only remedy is isolation.

Boo-fucking-hoo.

***

When new people or new situations—job, relationship, etc.—come into my life, there's a kind of understanding that it will fuck me up irreversibly in some way. I'll lose it on some level, and I'll become sick again.

Job after job, day and night, night and day, new people and new miseries to deal with. The most frustrating part of my existence is that nothing is permanent. Friends, jobs, moods: all in a constant state of flux. All of it hanging in the balance, waiting to drop, the other shoe, the left foot. Waiting for my life to fall apart again.

And so it was with Ken Allen, the man who I would like to think is not completely evil, but who is completely evil, no matter what he'll tell you, and he'll tell you for hours what a great guy he is.

He's only human, they'll say.

Everyone makes mistakes, they'll tell you.

That's why pencils have erasers, they'll say, saying it in such a patronizing tone that to rip their tongues out by the root would be too good for them.

But when it comes to me …

He's a liar, he's a whiner, he's a buzzkill, he's no fun to be around, he's angry all the time, who needs him? Who the fuck needs to be brought down all the time? Did you hear what he did? Did you hear what that fucking freak did? He calls it delusional; I call it lying! He's a liar, and he's so goddamn depressing to be around …

Wait. I'm not human? I don't make mistakes? Where's my fucking eraser?

But Ken …

Yes, now I recall.

The man comes into my life with that sardonic grin and chubby, mushroom head, flat face with eyes too far apart—Mother drank—and he walks in and my life is changed forever. No going back. Done deal.

Hi, I say to him, still under the impression that the man is human.

Yeah, I'm Ken. I read the ad in the Voice, wanted to know if the room was still available.

You should have called, I tell him. *I already have someone lined up to take it,* I say, watching his eyes burn through me—pokepokepoke.

I'll pay thirty dollars on top of whatever anyone else is paying you. I can't turn that down. He goes on with *I just got kicked out of my place.*(No need to ask why that was, right? Moron.)

Really? Well, when can you move in?

Tomorrow.

I'll need first and last month's rent up front.

No security?

Two hundred dollars.

The jackass fishes in his jacket pocket and pulls out a wad of bills, flips through them, hands me a clump of money and I still don't ask him about references, or prior landlords, or anything.

Next day, he moves in, and my life is shit in a shoe, and has remained shit in a shoe ever since.

***

The fridge should go over there, in the corner, against the wall next to the window, feng shui and shit, he tells me twenty-three minutes after bringing in the last of his five boxes. (All CDs, no books.)

Actually, I like it where it is.

Well, if you ever want more room in the kitchen, you'll do it.

I wanted to ask him what made him think I would, in fact, do anything he told me to do. But instead I said, *We'll see.*

***

He's sitting in my chair wearing nothing but boxer shorts. I can see his tiny, pen cap dick though the hole as he sits Indian style. I don't know if he knows I can see his twiddlecock, but if he does, he doesn't seem all that bothered by it. And if I had a cock as teenytiny as his,

I'd be bothered by it *huge* time. Did I mention that he's sitting in *my* chair? Fucker.

When I was four, my parents split up, and I was left to raise my sister. We lived in a tiny apartment in Beverly Hills. Tiny place.

Really? (Indifferent)

But then I got a job, a good one, and it changed my life!

What job? (Totally indifferent)

I became a personal assistant!

Really?

Guess who I was working for?

I guess.

No, guess again!

I guess again.

Jesus, you're way off.

Oh no.

I worked for Steve Fucking Buschemi!

Who?

Steve Buschemi. He was in The Big Lebowski.

The what Lebowski?

"Little guy? Kind of rat faced?" That's a line from Fargo.
He was in Fargo.

I'm going to bed.

I also worked under Vince Vaughn.

Was it hard to breathe?

Was what hard to breathe?

I'm going to bed. Turn off the light on your way out.

***

For the first week, he wanted to discuss family, he wanted to discuss the future, politics. But first and foremost, he wanted to discuss Me—Me with a capital *M*. All that was, is, and ever would be Me. He wanted to discuss every detail of my life, and oh did he!

You should never let anyone tell you that you're not good enough, man, he says.

There are things in life that you just have to go out and grab! he says.

I think you might be too attached to your mother …

Hold up. Wait, wait, wait, wait. What?

I think you—you know— think too highly of your mother. I mean, Christ, man! You're almost thirty years old and you still talk to her every day on the telephone.

I think you better shut up about my mom, Ken.

I think you need to hear this, man.

Shut the fuck up about my mother, okay?

Interesting …

What?

It's just interesting. Your mother complex. It's very interesting.

I informed Ken that if he ever talked about my mother again, he'd be homeless.

Again, he said, *Interesting.*

***

Alcohol got the best of me, said Ken one night—one of our many nights of deep talks that usually started around the time I got home from work till whenever I kicked him out of my room. He went on: *I just saw what was becoming of my life. Steve Buschemi fired me. I lost my apartment—*

I thought you lived with your—

Right, but I lost my apartment and then I was living on the street for a while.

I didn't have the heart to call him a liar.

***

When the sickness comes, when it grabs my head and seeps in through my nose and ears and mouth—when my mind turns to shit—my words become mumbles; I think of things from the past—my sister, my brother, my father, my mother—and suddenly I'm no longer me; I'm Me. Me with a capital *M*. *So what now,* I think to myself as The Brain turns to jelly—strawberry, raspberry, grape jam. Little bits of memory stuck inside like seeds in the preserves, nothing more, nothing more. And now and now and now I am no one and everyone, I am Me and Myself; I am him and her.

When I look out the window, I see the crazycrazy people—the *real* crazy people, the ones who call themselves Jesus Christ—those guys—the ones who call themselves Lucifer—those guys—the ones who mutter and grumble under bridges and entryways and in back alleys. Those guys.

I think back to when I was just a boy, just a little kid and there I was, with Suzie and Donald in the park or at the beach or at the—no!

Memories hit me of that day, that one day, with the spiders and the hand on the shoulder and I'm now half asleep in a gravel pit, half dreaming, half screaming, and my head caves in, and I look up and ask my mother where Suzie went. Mom doesn't know. *Probably went on ahead ...* But she did not go ahead. No, no! No, nonono! She's in a fucking garage being hurt and pokepokepoke. Someone help her!

It should have been me, I should have screamed, I should have done something—*anything!* I should have felt her hand fall off my shoulder. I should have heard some goddamn sound—

But I didn't.

And she's dead.

***

I wake up screaming. Ken rushes into the room and grabs my arms and shakes me awake—wide awake—and the back of my neck feels like someone has been spitting on it for much of the night—slick and sticky—but I won't stop screaming.

I'll never stop screaming.

***

Mr. Deets glares at me—been doing this for a week now. Just stands over my desk and glares at me, tries to intimidate me. (Succeeds)

Daren Pewterschmidt sits across from me and every few seconds will let his eyes wander over the desk to me, to my face, to my frightened look of scared bewilderment. What did I do? What did I do?

Yes—Yes! This is one!

Deets clears his throat.

He walks to my desk, bends down and leans in on his fingers. *You going to freak out again, Dolby?* (He leans in, lips brushing my earlobe, making my skin bristle.) *I'll fucking rip your ass to shreds, Dolby. And no one's going to save you this time.* (He glances at Daren, whose eyes haven't found their way to my desk.) *You're mine. You fuck up once and you're mine.*

(Call him a fucker! Call him a cocksucking motherfucking twat-headed mule fucker—anything but just sit there!)

Yes, sir. Thank you. (Pussy)

His eyes find their way over to Vivian Chance. He stares at her breasts the way a child eyes a candy bar. She notices and subtly covers the nape of her neck with her hand. Deets goes back to his office and leaves me alone to my neurosis and my fear of being fired.

***

I've had seven jobs in the past two years, three this year alone—this is my seventh job in thirty-seven months. I worked at the Ditmyer Agency. I worked at Walter Martin Publishing; Davis, Mullenburgh & Davis (publishing); Vicki Lawson Agency; Marsha Orleans, Inc.; the Franklin House. And finally, Daniels & Webster.

Each time I either find a reason to leave (paranoia, impetuousness, panic), or I am asked to leave. (*No ill feelings; you ever need a reference, you got one. Have a nice life, fuck you hard, and get out ...*)

This is the last job I'm going to take in the literary business. It took me seven years to finish college—I went to Albright College, UConn, Hunter College, Baruch College, and then Hunter, and then back to Baruch. Never finishing a goddamn thing seems to be my day job. I don't work in publishing; I quit in publishing and find new work. It's fun trying to pay rent and shit when you can't keep a job or stay in one fucking school for more than a year. Mind you, I did well in school. I was a decent student, keeping a 3.2 average for four of the six years. They have a label they give to someone who spends seven years going to college. They call them *doctors.*

I can't finish anything and I can't hold a job. I just can't.

When my mind is lucid, I'm manic. When my mind is sinking, it's very melancholic and airy. Lead in the chest. Bad dreams. Despair over nothing. I feel as if I'm dreaming. I hear things. I see things. I feel things. I want things. I know things. I hate things. I am things. I need things. I have things that make me do things I have little or no control over. (see: losing it in office)

I make no excuse for my behavior. But I shouldn't be judged by it, either. I am not my disease.

And it's not mind over matter.

And it's not a matter of mental strength.

And it's not about a *positive fucking attitude.*

My mind doesn't work right. If it did, I wouldn't need medication and I wouldn't be crazy. If my mind worked, yes, it would all be mental. But it doesn't, so fuck you and your fucking self-help mantras: you think I *enjoy* being like this?

You can't win.

They want you to fail.

And it's not about the power of the mind—it's about a mind that's ill, sick, disturbed, malfunctioning, destroyed, deteriorated. If I was in a car crash and suffered brain damage, there'd be sympathy. But living with this, I'm just plain, unadulterated, 100 percent nutty. I'm strange and scary and bothersome. And I'm frightened of myself beyond all hope. Terrified. Every. Single. Day.

You can't win.

They simply don't understand. And they never will. And there's nothing you can do about it but sit there and take it.

***

So, Ken has an alcohol problem—or did—and now I do as well, apparently. I know it sounds outlandish. *My* dad had a drinking problem, so therefore I do. But I don't have a drinking problem—not that I'm aware of—and I have, maybe, four beers in a week. Maybe a drink or two when going out, and now I'm a drunk and I'm ruining my life. So says Ken, omniscient, all-knowing Ken. Knows me like the back of his hand, reads me like a book, he does, after three weeks. Impressive.

And here he is, telling me that I have a problem.

I can see the signs, he says.

The signs?

The signs of alcoholism! he says. *My dad was a gin drinker—so was I—he used to beat us all pretty bad. He had the signs. I had the signs. And you, my friend, have the signs. Of alcoholism, I mean.*

Whatever, I say.

Hey, if you want to beat your children, whatever, but don't say I didn't warn you.

So, I say. *What are the signs? What* signs *do I have?* I ask him as he sips his Coca-Cola, pounds it down like a bum swills from a bottle of booze.

You drink alone.

I chuckle. *I only drink alone when no one is here. So prior to you moving in, I drank alone every time I drank. What's your point?*

Why drink alone? Drinking is a social function.

Says who? Drinking a beer at night once in a while is not a problem!

Anyway, drinking alone is a surefire way to develop the alcohol problem that I think you know you might have.

I shake my head and glare at him. *If I have a problem, then 3 billion other people have a problem as well. Drinking alone simply means there's no one else around when you drink.*

Hey, he says, *I can only show you the door; you have to open it.*

***

For a week he did this every fucking night. He did it when I drank, he even did it when I didn't drink. He almost had me convinced I actually had a problem, but the thing of it is, if you tell a man he's a chicken long enough, sooner or later he'll try to lay an egg.

So I went to a meeting just to shut him up. Seriously, it was almost unbearable and the thirty extra dollars a month was becoming less and less of a justification to have this bastard living with me. He never signed a lease. He was a squatter, basically, and there was nothing keeping him in his disgustingly filthy room, a room covered in dust, smelling of sweat and body odor, newspapers all over the floor with hamburger wrappers and all kinds of nasty shit. But there was nothing keeping him.

Anyway, the meeting I went to was full of deadbeats and losers. Bottom's a lonely place, even when there's a room full of people down there with you—people who made me feel much better about myself, I might add. My dad went to AA and it saved his life, but that doesn't mean everyone who drinks needs saving. For some—most—people, AA is the answer. And it's great if you work it and it works for you. My experience, however, was not good. I did not work it. I did not find my salvation. I did not need saving. Life is full of generalizations. No one and no thing is everyone and everything. Not all alcoholics are Ken, but not all drinkers are Ken, either. There are great people in AA, I'm sure. Most have their heads on straight. Most care about newcomers. Most are truly good people. But some are not good. But some are messed up, and take advantage of people who don't know any better. Go to the meetings if you need saving. But don't drag me along for the ride.

***

The meeting I go to is in the basement of an old tenement building on Bleecker Street. Ken wanders off to flirt with an older woman while I'm stuck by the coffeemaker with a man named Ted. (*Hello, Ted ...*)

We start talking. I tell him that I'm in publishing. I tell him that I'm seeing someone. I tell him this and that; small trifles no one would remember. Then, for reasons beyond me, I tell him that I'm mentally ill.

You taking medication?

I know I was giving him a funny look. *Um, yes ...some medication.*

He shakes his head despairingly—as if I just admitted something awful about myself. Like I just told him I fuck grapes.

Son, psychotropic drugs are kind of what we're fighting against here at AA. It alters the mind. What's the difference between mind-altering drugs and mind-altering intoxicants?

I'm speechless. Absolutely speechless.

I would strongly recommend you get off that shit. Seriously.

I'm not sure that would be a good idea. I get psychotic.

It's worth it to be sober. (Unreal)

I stare. I turn. I walk away.

***

That night, Ken asks me what I thought of the meeting.

I can think of at least seven things I would have rather done on a Saturday …

He laughs patronizingly. *Right, right. But what did you think of the meeting itself?*

I thought about that putz, Ted. *Is it true that taking medication is wrong?*

The Big Book says, "We are not physicians." *Some take that meaning literally—like you can't tell people to stop taking their medication. And some say that it simply means we can't fix people. That we are only able to help ourselves.*

And what do you believe?

He doesn't answer. Instead he tells me that I should go to ninety meetings in ninety days.

Why?

Because, that's what people in recovery do.

What am I recovering from?

Alcoholism! What the hell are we talking about?

I don't have a problem with alcohol.

God, he says. *You sound so cliché right now. Poster child shit.*

I tell him he's got no fucking right to make claims like that, let alone plan the next ninety days of my life. I

Lithium*buzz*

tell him to go to hell. Then physically throw him out of my room.

35

THREE: *Stop Bleeding on My Carpet*

I was watching *Diff'rent Strokes* on Nick at Nite. It was the episode where Gary Coleman and his brother Willis drop plastic bags filled with water out the window of their apartment, hitting people on the head. He learns a valuable lesson about maturity, or responsibility, or ethics (I didn't care at the time. I still don't) by the end of the episode. I'm watching the episode and—holy hell!—I have a beer in my hand, opened a half hour before the door opens, and Ken walks into the apartment. The bottle is still half full after thirty minutes.

Yes! Now I—

Right. Uh—Yes!

No—wait.

He disappears inside his pit for a few moments, and then walks into my room dressed in shorts. And that's it. Just shorts, baring his flabby, pasty chest and everything else God gave him hanging out every whichway. He eyes me, he eyes what I'm holding, looks at me again, the beer, then me, smiling, he says, *Ah, drinking alone* yet again …

I am, I said. *I didn't know when you'd be home so I started without you. My bad.*

You sure you don't have a problem?

Fuck off, Ken.

No, I think you need to hear this, I—

Ken. I said fuck off.

He sits down in my chair—*my chair*—and sighs heavily: like a frustrated mother. *You can't talk to me like that, man. You can't. I'm trying to help you out and you show me no respect.*

Well, Godfather, I didn't know that was required in my apartment.

Your *apartment? Hey,* he says, *this is my apartment, too!*

It is? Funny, I didn't see your name on the lease …

Renters' rights, he says. *I have renters' rights,* he tells me. Then adds for effect: *Renters'. Rights.*

Get out of my room, I say. *Get the fuck out of here right now!* (What's that? Do what?)

Don't talk to me like that. I mean it.

Get out of my fucking room, Ken! (No, maybe you shouldn't do that to him.)

He yells (drama queen), *Why are you drinking alone? Why are you—*

Look, I tell him real slow and loud-like, as if talking to a bad puppy, *I was drinking alone because you weren't here. And you have a choice: you can either watch me drink it, or you can simply walk out of here and let me watch the encore presentation of* Diff'rent Strokes *in peace—it's your call!*

He looks at me. He smiles. He cocks his head to the side and smiles smiles smiles …

What the fuck is your deal? I ask him in a drawl.

Interesting … he says.

What's interesting? What the fuck *is so* fucking *interesting, Ken?*

You. You're interesting.

Then it happened. I grabbed my bottle and I smacked Ken (rather lightly) across the forehead with it, grazing him slightly. He looked at me. He blinked twice. Then he fell to the floor in a clump, leaving me to wonder if I'd just killed the fat son of a bitch.

But then, then he starts to bleed. I reel a little, glancing around the room, out the window, as if someone might be watching me—saw what I did—and I need to get him into the tub so he'll stop bleeding on my carpet. After a fuckload of effort, I toss him in and start to panic. Running to the hallway cabinet, I take out an old ripped-up towel that I can throw away without remorse, go to the bathroom, and wrap it around Ken's mushroom head.

He bled a little for forty-five minutes, then woke up, then threw the towel at me and told me he was leaving.

Oh God, no …

***

His shit was gone two days after the "bottle incident." I was getting ready to go to my psych appointment when the buzzer to my building rang—a loud obnoxious drone, the kind of bullhorn sound you would expect from a prewar tenement shamble such as my own—and going to answer it, I peeped out the window, hiding my head behind the curtain, and saw there, parked at the curb, a patrol car with flashing lights twirling about the top, casting blue and white and red blips on my wall. The buzzer buzzed again. Again and again until I cursed and found my way to the door, obviously expecting cops to appear behind it.

The door was opened and they showed me a warrant and I let them in.

Mr. Dolby? said one of them, dressed in Columbowear—trench and rumpled slacks, askew tie that didn't match the outfit whatsoever.

Yes?

We need to ask you a few questions.

Oh my God, I said. *Is he dead?*

The two officers glanced at each other, then the one stared at Columbo, waiting for him to tell me what I already knew: Ken was found dead underneath the Manhattan Bridge with thirty-seven bullet wounds covering his body. But I was wrong.

Mr. Ken Allen came to us yesterday with minor head wounds, claiming that you, sir, wounded him. Is that so? Because that would be assault and battery, my friend.

Look, I told the two men, *he was provoking me. He was deliberately trying to goad me into a reaction. He—*

You're under arrest, sir; you have the right to remain silent, anything you say or do— Blah blah blah …

Apparently, Ken had told the men handcuffing me that I had attacked him in a drunken rage. That was obviously a half-truth. He also implied that he'd almost died. In the cop car, I tried explaining that the beer was my first. Again telling them that Ken was provoking me—picking a fight just to get a rise out of me. At the station, the detective questioned me, then told me that I would be getting a summons shortly. He then informed me off the cuff that if I went to AA meetings, the judge might be lenient come sentencing.

I fucking hate irony.

***

The dream I dream is crammed full of joy and love and the warmwarm sun. I dream the dream often, not too often, but often enough to make my stomach turn to flame and fire, waking me with the feeling I've done something irreversibly wrong, though I've done nothing. Nothing at all, but dream a dream I always dream. And it's of her.

I dream of Suzanne.

She wakes me. She shakes me awake at six in the morning, telling me to runrun with her to the river, where we can watch the sunrise, just the two of us, me and her, and we'll watch it rise and rise and rise, then talk about Mom and Dad and dumb Donald. She always laughs when I say things about Donald, and I know it doesn't bother her that I say things about him, even though they're almost the same age and are real close. Like friends almost. He's almost eleven. She'll be fourteen in July. I'm still just a little kid, and when she turns fourteen, I'm real worried she won't like doing things with me as much because she'll be older. We won't go to the river anymore. It'll be just me and the sun, and no more Suzie once she turns fourteen.

But we know she never makes it that long. No. Still a girl when she dies. The blood. The redred blood that trickles down her arms and into the bathtub in the basement of our house on Walnut Street. Our blue house. The one we painted the year that the man in tweed came and kissed my mother. The man in tweed is still kissing my mother. Bastard Dexter.

My father alone. My father drunk half the time, but still alone and weary and sick. And Mother says she loves him, just not *in* love, she says, and I wonder what that means, even these days—even in the days of the dreams I wonder what that means.

***

We're at the river and the sun rises like a glowing yellow quarter, hanging above First Federal Bank, the bank put up last year. The bank no one goes to because it's where the old Assembly of God church used to be, and to go there is blasphemy. But we're goddamn Catholics, so Mom and Dad go there. The sun over it now, just sitting there. I try not to stare into it, but fail miserably and close my eyes, still seeing the green imprint of it on my eyelids.

Suzie puts her arm around me.

Are you ready for the zoo? she asks me in a voice that makes me feel very warm and cozy. *You'll see the penguins.*

I nod, eyes closed, seeing the orange glow of the sun on my eyelids.

Why do you love penguins so much?

I shrug.

Is it because they can swim?

Shake head. Open eyes. Take another look at the sun. Close them.

I speak: *They can't fly away,* I tell her.

***

Mother never speaks of Suzanne. She's the forgotten child Mom never had. No one talks about her anymore.

But there'll always be a corner of my mind for my sister. A corner that isn't tainted by madness. It's hers forever.

Yes. Do it. Remember her.

***

I wake up suddenly, again shaking and sweaty, my stomach aching. I throw the sheets onto the floor and make my way to the door of my room. Opening the door, I half expect to see Ken's light on. He never really slept, it seemed. I go to the bathroom and take my medication—effexor for the mood, bupropion for the floor, and lamotrigine for the ceiling. Taking them is a fucking ordeal. Horse pills in a wide variety of fun colors. Choke them down, go back to bed, and for some reason, feel very scared.

I actually miss Ken. And that's the worst feeling of all.

FOUR: *This Is When Things Started Getting a Bit Fuzzy ...*

I remember Mother holding my—

Wait.

No. God no.

Suzie sitting at the riverside with the sun, a warmwarm glowing quarter—

No! Just—no wait!

How about—wait—Yes!

The garage is cramped and small and it looks like no one has stepped foot in it in years, save my sister, who was found in the upper attic of the small structure, among the boxes and old fishing rods. Ronny Feldham was not at home when the police arrived. He was at church, St. Martin's Lutheran Church, where he was directing the choir as they sang "A Mighty Fortress Is Our God," as the police knocked on the door of his small house.

The instant I heard she was alive and well it was about 11:00 in the morning. We hadn't gone to mass because Mom refused to talk to God anymore, Goddamn it! and there was no consoling her even after they found my sister.

Yes! I rem—

Wait—

Could this be—

The air conditioner in our house blows mist into the living room, cat hair dancing in the air above my nose. Try to grab it, but it slips through my fingers. Then Dad walks in with a strange look—a weary look—the kind he has all the time now. The look just being born then. Attaching itself to his face.

He comes into the room and says they've found her, that she's—

Wait—

Yes! Yesyesyes!

The Freak looks at his three friends, Mike and Pat and Keith, and the three of them look at the Freak. The Freak is crying—I'm weeping; they glare and one of them says, *For the love of Christ …*

Fucking-A, man, what the fuck is it now?

Fucking buzzkill.

Jesus, Dolby, when's this shit gonna stop?

But I don't want to tell them. I don't want to tell Mike and Pat and Keith the reason I'm crying, that it's the anniversary of Suzie and that I miss her. Because they'll harass me. Why do I stay? Why do I stay here with these meanmean guys, the bullies? They are the only ones, that's why. They're the only ones who will let me go with them when they drink or smoke or sneak out at night to meet girls.

But they're so mean—

I miss my sister, I mumble. Hope they don't hear.

Your sister? says Mike, says it with such incredulity you'd think I just confessed that I like stapling baloney to my chest. Mike glances at Keith, Keith at Pat. *What sister?* says Mike. *You don't have a fucking sister!* says Mike.

So goddamn cruel.

God, you are such a fucking buzzkill, says Pat. *Every time we go out, you sit there like a fucking lump and whine or cry about something. I've had it!*

So they leave me. So they go off to do what they do, and they leave me alone with Myself—Me with a capital *M.*

***

I remember—wait—yes!

Wait.

Do I? Yes! Yes I—

I remember the whitewashed walls, the paint smelling of death—old clothes and aftershave—and I stand over the casket and wish she would open her eyes and smile and say, *Just kidding!* as she did when I would hit her with a baseball or football in the face, and she'd fall over, pretend to be knocked unconscious, and then open her eyes and smile and say that—say, *Just kidding.*

Her eyes pasted shut, she doesn't look so much dead as she looks plasticized: Suzie Q, frozen, shiny, her wrists covered by her purple shirtsleeve. I can't believe this is what she's going to wear for all eternity. They should have told Suzie what she would be buried in. She may have reconsidered.

***

It was the day I was supposed to go to the AA meeting—any AA meeting—to help me with my lawsuit. To make the judge more lenient on me, think I'm a good 'n sober guy who would never get looped and smash a bottle over some poor fat bastard's head. Getting up, taking meds, jumping in the shower, I realize that I'm the only one here, I'm the last man standing! I shout, *Yeah, I win I win I win!* for no real reason other than the fact that I feel like screaming it. Getting out, drying, there is a message on my machine from my brother Donald. He called while I was showering.

Hey, buddy, it's me. Just checking up on you, seeing how everything's panning out these days. Haven't heard from you.

Mom tells me you haven't called her for a while—you might do that. Anyway, call me. Later.

Click—

Dial tone.

Alone again.

It's a Saturday and I have off, and I also have an hour to kill, so I call my mother and wait for the inevitable to happen. When it does—right off the bat—I'm rather impressed. Usually it takes at least three or four statements to get into the manipulative nagging.

Jeepers H. Crap! Did you forget that you even had a mother? My God, I was so worried! You have no idea what that's like for a mother to not know what her son is doing. With things the way they are and all, I thought you'd call me. I mean, is that too much to ask. For the love of Golly!

Mom, I say. *Mom, calm down. I'm fine. Donald called this morn—*

Did you talk to him?

Finishing, Mom. He called, but I was in the—

Where were you?

Shower.

What did you do last night?

Out.

Out where?

With Marianne.

Marianne?

Yes, Mom, my girlfriend, Marianne.

When did this happen?

When did what happen?

Fuck this. I change the subject and we talk about how awful things are for a while, then discuss my doctor: is she doing me any good, should I continue to see her? And then she tells me that she's going to the shore with Dexter in an hour and she has to go. *But I love you,* she says. *I really do,* she says.

Marianne calls me and I whine about my family, about how no one listens to me, even when I tell them something time and time again (see: Marianne). She doesn't say much and I'm afraid I've hurt her feelings by telling her that no one in my family remembers her. I mention that Suzanne would have. Marianne tells me that Suzanne wasn't like the others in my family. She had her head on straight. She was a perfect sister, Suzanne was. And I love her.

Marianne wishes me luck at my meeting and asks if we can go out later. *Please,* she says, *please? I need to see you.*

It feels nice to be needed.

***

On the train going into the city, reading an old copy of *The Crucible* that I still have from high school—I stole it from the school library senior year, that's how much I love that play—I notice a man across the way glancing at me and then down at the book I'm reading. The book still has *Property of Glenview Park High School* stickered on the front cover. The man, about my age and vaguely familiar, clears his throat. Tries to get my attention. Succeeds.

Excuse me …

I finish the dialogue I'm reading and look up.

Excuse me? Did you go to Glenview High, by chance? he asks.

I nod, turn my attention back to the play. He clears his throat again and I realize that I'm being rude. And I don't care. But I look at him anyway and tell him, *Yes, I did about twelve years ago.*

You're name isn't Dolby, is it?

I nod. I look at him, and then realize that I'm looking at Keith Mann. Friend, fiend, foe. He smiles huge and shakes his head.

Oh my God! It can't—Jesus, it's been, what?

Twelve years, I tell him.

I feel very uncomfortable. I've hated this guy for so long. And here he is. It's like the dream you have—if you're like me—where you're with friends from high school or college. Friends who always dicked you around and you finally get to tell them how you really feel. Tell them to go fuck themselves with a long pole, and, for some reason, you always say the right thing in your dream. You always—*always*—say the right thing, and here I am, looking at this prick from the past and wondering what the fuck I'm supposed to tell him.

You look fantastic! he says. He shakes his head for effect. *You look really great.* He gets up and walks over to me, sits down. *What are you up to? Jesus, the odds, huh?*

It's a mind fuck all right.

Yeah, I say. *What are the odds?*

How are you? What have you been up to? Are you doing any better?

(Tell him to cram it hard! Tell him to eat shit and fucking die bleeding on the street! Tell him that you're fucking his mom!) *I'm doing great. Working in publishing at the moment. Just surviving.*

God, he says in a hush. *We never thought you'd make it …*

Who?

We. You know. The guys.

So fucking what?

Really? I ask. *You never thought I'd make it?*

He shakes his head. *We thought you'd end up in your mom's basement.*

Sorry to disappoint.

No, no! That's a good thing—I mean, it's great what you're doing! I mean it!

Jesus fucking—

What are you doing right now? he says.

Riding the subway with a fucking tool. You?

Nothing, I say. *I have a meeting at two that I'm going to.*

Oh. Right. Good, good. Well, do you want to get some coffee? I'm in the city for a convention this weekend. I live up in Scranton with my wife. And a daughter. I'm in chiropractics!

(What do they call a med student who flunks out of med school …? Give up?)

Wonderful, I mutter, real sarcastic-like. He doesn't pick up on it. Idiot.

Let's get some coffee? Please tell me you can get some coffee. Or a drink!

It's eleven in the morning, I tell him. *Coffee will be fine.*

***

At a small place on Hudson street called Manny's, the two of us sit down with coffee and croissants. He starts eating loudly—smackingslurpingsighing—because we all know what a fucking ordeal it can be to eat a goddamn croissant! There's food pasted to his chin. Disgusting. I wait for the revulsion to pass. When it does, I ask him how he's been.

And he tells me. For two hours.

***

And you? he asks me, seemingly hell bent on getting me to admit that things are shitty. Shitty and pasty all over.

I'm good. Like I said, I'm doing fine. I work at Daniels & Webster Publishing. Good job. Seeing someone—

Details, please … he says, smoothly, like we're old girlfriends.

Well, do you remember Marianne?

He says nothing. Makes no move. Doesn't respond.

You know, Marianne?

Oh, he says. *Right, Marianne. Right.*

I nod.

He says, *Sweet, man.*

There's something odd going on here and I can't put my finger on it.

***

He'll be in town for a couple of days, and then he's off to Scranton again. But I should call him, or, better yet,

Email me, how's that? because hearing my voice means that we're actually communicating.

He gives me his card. He says goodbye. I leave. I wander over to Bleecker Street and find the church the AA meeting is in, and go inside.

***

Tell a man he's a chicken long enough, and sooner or later he'll try to lay an egg.

I get to the meeting and there's already a room full of men and women waiting to get sober. Ted is there, standing in the corner with a smile and a wave; he comes over to me and slaps me on the back so hard I feel my heart stop.

Hey! Dolby, right?

Yeah, Ted. How are—

Damn good to see you here. Did you get off the shit yet? Ready to get sober?

I'm not sure if that's a good idea—

Getting sober is the best idea out there; don't let no one tell you otherwise.

Would you tell a guy with diabetes to stop taking insulin, Ted?

No, of course not. Why?

Just wondering.

We talk a while about this and that—my drug problem, mainly—when who should I see walk into my life once again but Ken Allen. Woo-hay! I tell Ted I need to use the men's room, and start walking along the side of the room, brushing past other men and women. One guy can't be more than sixteen. I come to the doorway, the stairs still full of people coming down into the room, and Ken walks right by me without seeing me. Unfortunately, my foot is sticking out a snad too far and he trips. Oh! Did I mention he's carrying crutches? Well, he is. How he got his head mixed up with his leg is beyond me. Maybe I *did* hit him too hard.

Shit! he hisses as he falls to the floor.

I make my way up the stairs, listening to people gasp and curse and chuckle.

As I reach the top of the stairs, I hear, *People—people, this is the man who did this* (points to legs and head) *to me. I was sitting in the apartment we shared and he attacked me in a drunken rage.* (How recited is this shit?) *But I forgive him …*

Oh! That's why you sic the cops on me, Ken? Because you forgive me?

He chuckles. *Interesting,* he says.

What?

Just …interesting.

And that's when it happens. Just as Ken starts up telling the AAers about W*hat kind of bums are we letting* *into the rooms these days?* Just as he starts up with that I feel my neck stiffen. There's a *buzzbuzzbuzz* sound in my ear. (Go on. Do it. You can. You should. Do it. Go on ...) The voices in the room get cloudy. I hear, *Oh my God!* I hear, *Someone should stop this!* I hear, *Oh my good gosh! Get that man off the cripple!*

I can vaguely hear people laughing screaming gasping as I jump on that fat son of a bitch and grab hold of his neck and won't let go. My soul seems to hover over the two bodies on the floor—notmine orhis. Someone else there on the floor strangling Ken. Who isn't Ken, just some fat guy. Some extra. Dies off in the first scene. No one misses him.

Then my soul creeps back into my body. I can't hear a damn thing. Just the muffled sounds of shouting. Then hands on me. A slap on the head. And then ...

Nothing.

It all goes black.

***

I woke up in a bed with a harness around my torso and my hands tied down with leather belts. My legs, too. I screamed. When a nurse finally came, I begged for some water. She said I couldn't have any. She wouldn't give me a reason why. She just walked away. I looked to my right and saw another unfortunate soul with a gaping hole in his stomach that looked like spaghetti and Ragu. To my left was a man who at some point in the evening probably had a large knife sticking out of his chest. He was unconscious. I called for a nurse again. Spaghetti Sauce Man told me to shut up. I ignored him and called again, loudly. A nurse came. She was carrying a syringe and poked my arm with the needle a few times, hit the vein, and then squirted something into my body. Black. When I woke, I was in a small room with white walls and a white bed with white sheets and I honestly thought I was in heaven.

I was not. My face was broken. My hands were sore and bleeding. I heard screaming. I was in a mental hospital.

No! Stoppit stoppit! Get away from—

By Thursday, I was released.

***

Dr. Sprat is very pretty in a pert, squat sort of way. Her nose is long, her eyes spaced asymmetrically apart, her chin pushed way in, her upper cleft pulled way out. She has a thin frame, and is very pretty in that kind of cute way. She has been my psychiatrist for years. Since I moved to New York.

So, you're seeing … Marianne? she asks me, looking confused. (Confused?)

Yes. Marianne.

For how long? Where did you meet?

Oh. A library. We met at the Public Library. The one in the East Village, and we … (I tell her the story) *And we've been together ever since.*

58

Huh.

What?

I'm getting angry.

Let's move on … How have you been feeling?

***

When I first started seeing her, she initially thought I had a borderline personality disorder. I was treated as such until that Wonderbread diagnosis proved somewhat inaccurate, being that I was standing on the platform at Eighth Street and saw a mouse run across my line of vision. Then another. Then another. Anotherandanother andanother.

I screamed and ran and caused something of a panic.

They're almost twins, borderline personality disorder and bipolar disorder, manic-depression for the layman. They're almost alike. Almost. *Almost.* You hold them up and they look alike. You've got the paranoia. You've got the moody shit—updownupdown. You've got anger and anxiety. You have the impulsive, manic behavior. You're really fucking unstable and in both cases there is a high risk of suicide and self-inflicted injury. You've got everything lined up in two neat rows and the symptoms look alike, see? However—and this is a big *however!*—with bipolar disorder comes psychosis. And that, my friend, has nothing to do with personality.

And everything had been somewhat fine until meeting that fatfuck bastard Ken, going to that fucking AA meeting, and bashing him over the head with a bottle! I was shipped to St. Mark's—the white-walled hospital— the Burger King of mental wards. I spent two full days fending for myself, trying to keep the freaks at bay, and then went to see Sprat and she put me on some different medication.

I was put on haldol and clonazepam. She said she was concerned. (Concerned?) This on top of my other happymeds.

Happyhappyhappy.

Sanesanesane.

This was when things started getting a bit fuzzy.

FIVE: *Keep on Trucking ...*

Marianne calls and I go out with her. I go out with her a lot.

Once a week, I go to a new AA meeting, a new place every time I go, usually uptown. Upper West Side. There everyone is medicated anyway, so I won't have to hear about how I'm a druggie because I don't want to see tiny mice running every whichway while I hear Ghandi telling me, *By the grace of Vishnu, I was mistaken ...Kill everybody!*

So, there I am, at a meeting at Holy Mary Mother of God Church on West End and it's my turn to talk. They come to me and I say my name. So I guess I have to tell them my story.

I'm not sure what to say, I tell them. *I mean, technically I almost killed someone.* Everyone nods like they feel my pain, know what I'm going through—been there, done that. Killed a guy? Who hasn't? After the meeting, a man named Roger comes up and introduces himself (*Hello, Roger, etc., etc.*), and then tells me that my story is fascinating. That he wants to know if I'd share at the next meeting. I tell him I'd have to think about it, that I'm new to the rooms, that I don't feel comfortable in my new skin—my sober skin. He gives me a look, and I think I've said something wrong. So I just agree to share and walk off.

As I get to the door, a woman, Grace, tells me that I'm an inspiration, and that my story is a powerful one, and I should keep on trucking, she says.

Keep on truckin', buddy! she says.

I nod, leave, and decide I will never attend another AA meeting for as long as I live.

***

Marianne calls me later that evening to tell me that she's crazy about me. That she's never loved anyone more than she loves me. That she wants me forever. That she can't stop thinking about me. That I'm one in a million. That I'm golden.

That's good, (I think to myself) *really, really nice ...*

I love you, too, I tell her. *I love you,* I say.

She says it back, says it twice, as if I didn't hear her the first time. And I act like I didn't. Because I like to hear it.

***

Mother running down the hallway, knocking the lamp over, almost nudging me down the stairs as the phone rings in the hallway next to the door. The door that always makes a creakcreak sound when the hinges are raped by the rust that covers them. The phone rings and mother runs and almost knocks me down the stairs. Then she picks up the phone and in breathless hisses she speaks.

Leave us alone! she rasps, with a voice that sounds like sandpaper on raw meat. She stops. She puts her hand to her head. She shakes her head. She bites her lip. She nods her head. She mouths a swear word. The hands of the clock seem to tick backwards. There is a dead fish in the tank being eaten by the other ones. A tetra. Small fishy. Teenytiny fishy. Dead like my sister.

She sighs she bites her lip she squints she can't believe it could they really be saying this to her the audacity the fucked-up world we live in she—

Wait. No—yes!

I think—

Yes, yesyes! Now I know—

The newspaper flops to the bottom step after being tossed by Gregory the newspaper boy. Gregory used to play with me and now makes fun like all the rest, but still smiles and says hello when he throws papers at me. The paper has a picture of Suzie on the front and a headline that is bent underneath the paper and so all I can read are the cut-off words: "DOL DEAD PURP." Long headline, makes me angry for some reason that has nothing to do with Suzie being dead. I don't like the idea of other people knowing my sister. I don't like sharing her. I don't like anyone knowing who she is. I hide the paper and Mom sees me and she says, *What are you doing?*

Hiding the paper.

Why? Why are you—

I run away to the river where the sun used to rise like a shiny coin, but doesn't now; now it just sits there like some fucking sun-dried apricot and shifts with the passing hours. Never rises anymore.

Wait.

Yes! Now I—

Wait.

No. That didn't—

The man from the paper comes to the door and asks to talk to my father. He knows my mother is gone. It's been two months. The Mets are in the World Series. *The Sox seem pretty strong,* Dad always says between breaths, between gulps, between sucks from the bottle.

The man from the newspaper comes to the door and asks for my dad. And my dad is asleep in the other room. The man from the paper wonders if he could ask some questions. I say sure, even though my mother always tells me not to talk to strangers. Especially now. Mother comes by the house every day at four until six, to see me and Donald. She left a while ago. It's dark out. The man from the newspaper is getting nervy.

Look, kid. I just want to talk to your dad. Is he home or not?

I say he is. But sleeping.

Then he asks if he can talk to me.

I say sure.

He asks me what my sister was buried in. I tell him it was a purple dress with long sleeves. He asks me if the long sleeves were because of the wrists. I ask him what he means. He says that she slit her wrists. *She slit her wrists,* he says. *Right? I mean, that was in the release.*

What's a release?

Never mind. So, she wore a purple dress. And what else? he says. I tell him. *If Ronny Feldham was here right now, what would you say to him?* I tell him what I'd say. *Do you miss your sister?* he says. I tell him. He goes.

The next day comes and Gregory smiles and tries whacking me with the news and the headline is of Suzie. I want to hide it because then my mom and dad will know I talked to the newspaper man when they said never to talk to anyone with a pen and pad. I run to the river and throw it in, but it floats. The sun is behind me, stinking like a piece of fucking fruit and the paper just sits there on top of the water, bobbingbobbingbobbing. I throw stones at it. But it just floats. I throw lots of stones but it just floats. Lotsandlots of stones and it just sits there.

The next morning I walk to the river—yes!—walk to the river and see that the paper has disappeared. And it makes me think of my sister.

I cry.

***

I go to work and Deets isn't there. I'm told by Pewterschmidt that his wife died last night. I don't know what to feel just now. I feel the way you do when someone tells you they had to put their dog down—that his or her aunt died. You just don't quite know what to feel: sadness, pity, glee?

And so I decide to feel nothing.

Work is a day filled with me glancing over my shoulder at Deets's office, feeling his absent eyes on me, like phantom pains. His eyes bore into me from the seventh floor of First Presbyterian, or St. Luke's, or wherever he is. His telepathic hatred is almost too much—pokepokepoke—and I want to leave. At lunch, I go out with Pewterschmidt and he tells me that Deets's wife had the cancer for many years. And that was why Deets is such a rat bastard.

I finally allow myself to feel sorry for Deets, although I still hate him.

I spent that afternoon putting twos on aces, threes on twos, and queens on kings on my computer solitaire. There were at least five manuscripts to peruse, but I had other things to worry about. Such as how the hell I was going to get the four at the bottom of the deck on the three in the hearts pile being that I couldn't move the two cards on top of it.

You think you have problems.

***

Marianne has work tonight. She works late some nights. She is an accountant and works in the Trade Center in the North Tower. She's always getting hit on by her co-workers. I hate that. But I know she loves me because she always tells me that she loves me. Always telling me things like, *I need you!* And, *You are my reason!* And, *I love you more than life itself, you know that, don't you, baby?*

She had work, so I went out for drinks with some people from work who I didn't really know, and so while they all got tanked and their voices got louder and louder, I got drunk and got quieter and quieter. They started talking loudly; I shrank into the corner. Smiled at something mildly amusing now and then, but generally just stayed the hell out of the way.

I drank and then I started feeling depressed. I started thinking about my sister, about the fact that she'd probably be a mother by now. I'd be an uncle. And now my nephews or nieces don't exist. They never would. And so I started to cry. Everyone looked at me cross-eyed; they wondered, What the fuck? *Why is he—is he crying?* someone asks.

I don't—who is that?

I think that's—Dolby? Is that his name?

Is he the one who freaked out on Deets?

Who invited him? What's he doing here anyway?

I didn't invite him. Did you, Bloom?

Hell no.

Is he okay? should we call someone?

My God, he's really falling apart over there.

Thankfully, Pewterschmidt was there and he said he'd get me home. We left and I told him that I was feeling under the weather and I needed sleep. He asked if I wanted to go to his place and sleep there, that there was a pull-out bed and I could rest. I said I'd be fine. He insisted on taking me to my place so we got on a Brooklyn-bound R and sat in silence until we passed Whitehall Street. Under the East River, he told me that people at work were talking. He told me that people wanted to know what the fuck? They weren't nosey, he said, but they wanted to know why I talk to myself, why I mumble, why I tick, why I grin and smile at nothing, why I shake my head in amusement at jokes no one says, why I grit my teeth, why I shake sometimes, why my mouth moves and nothing comes out sometimes, why I don't talk to anyone. Why do I leave without saying goodbye? Why I come in without saying hello? Why am I such a recluse, such an enigma, why am I such a freak?

In my drunken state, I tell him that I'm manic-depressive, and naturally, he has no fucking clue what that means. So I tell him it means I'm a manicdepressive and that manic-depression can make you mumble stuff, talk to yourself, tick, grin and smile at nothing, shake your head in amusement at jokes no one says, grit teeth, shake, move mouth, etc., etc. He still doesn't understand.

So I tell him that I can't control my moods.

He doesn't get it.

So I tell him that I get manic.

He doesn't get it.

I get really depressed and really—I guess you'd call it hyper.

He doesn't get it.

I get happy and sad really fast.

He doesn't get it.

Never mind, I say.

Why can't you just tell yourself to be happy all the time? I don't get it.

I know, I feel like saying. No one does, you fucking ignorant prick.

***

Marianne came over last night and we made love for the last time. Today, I leave the apartment with Marianne, we get breakfast, she gets on the train, and I go and face Ken one last time.

SIX: *Monument to Stupidity*

Mr. Lupner, my attorney, stands with his back to me. He's talking to someone. I can't see his face, but his arms are moving madly, like a windmill that's lost its mind. Crazy motions, jabbing, cutting. I walk up to him as if in slow motion. I walk up to him, and he turns and smiles and I see who he's talking to. That shit-eating bastard Ken! That fat, tubby, pasty-skinned, fucknut, needledick, lardass cocksucker Ken Allen. He's smiling at me; mindfucking me. I glare as hard as I can, and then realize that it's not hurting him at all. That it's making him stronger. He's giving me that *interesting* look. He's about to say it. So help me, Christ, I'll kill him!

We were just talking, says Lupner. *I was just talking to Ken's lawyer an hour ago, and just told Old Ken here* (Old Ken here?) *what the two of us were talking about. Ken, would you excuse us for a moment?*

Sure, Bruce, says Ken. He smiles.

Sure, Bruce? I say. (Client confidentiality, what? What was that again?)

Ken saunters off and Lupner, nee Bruce, says to me, *I was talking with Mr. Allen's lawyer and we agree: we should either plead guilty or plead insanity.*

(What. The. Fuck.)

I mean, think about it, you attack a guy for no—

He provoked *me! Goddamn it, Mr. Lupner! The guy is fucking evil wrapped up in a polyester suit two sizes too small!*

Doesn't matter. You attacked him. Drunk, no less.

I wasn't drunk. (Don't attack your lawyer.)

Your word against his … (Do *not* attack your lawyer.)

Let's just do this, I say.

We go in. Ken's lawyer eyes me, smiles politely, whispers something to that fat fuck Ken. Ken nods as he smiles and looks my way. Nods again and says something quietly to the lawyer. The lawyer shakes his head and grins. They both shake their heads. Look at me. Ken smiles. I want to kill him so badly. It's important that I kill him. I have to do it or I'll die.

The hearing begins.

***

Long story short.

Instead of doing the stenographer's job and giving you a play-byplay, I'll make it quick. We start. I talk. Ken talks. The detective talks. Lupner talks. Ken's lawyer talks. The judge interrupts and asks the lawyers to approach the bench. They whisper. Ken smiles smiles smiles at me and I squint my eyes and glare as hard as I can and come to the same realization as before. He must die. The lawyers come back to their respective clients and they start whispering. Lupner says, *Hey, you're in luck!*

That's when I hear Ken hiss, *Sonuvabitch!*

And the judge clears his throat. And the judge asks us to stand. And the case is thrown out.

***

I shake hands with Lupner despite myself. I say thank you for saving my ass and he nods and goes over to talk to Ken's lawyer. Ken breaks off from the crowd and strides over to me.

You think this is over?

I say nothing. I want to say something—*anything! Christ!*—but nothing comes out. It's so frustrating to want to say something so badly and have nothing come to mind. A few options do come to mind, however (*Fuck you,* or, *Fuck you and die,* or, *Fuck off, fuckhead*), but still, nothing comes out.

I'm going to appeal this until I see you hanging by the balls, my friend.

I say nothing. God damn it, I say absolutely nothing!

You're going to crash and burn, you shit, he drawls.

I look at him. I open my mouth. I take a breath and think of what I'm going to say to him. Just as I start to speak—still not certain what's going to come out—he turns and walks off.

I'm left with nothing.

He walks away, and I never see or hear from him again.

***

Dr. Sprat sees me and I'm rather pissed off at the outcome of the hearing. Not that I mind being let off the hook for doing absolutely nothing outside of having a goddamn reaction to negative stimuli. I'm more or less disgusted with the way I left things with that mushroom-headed jerk-off Ken.

I want him dead!

Sprat glances at me and says, *You do know that if I feel you are a threat to yourself or others I have to report you, right?*

I was kidding.

I wasn't.

She informs me that she wants to put me on new medication. She tells me that with all the *negative stimuli*

I'm experiencing, my symptoms may become exacerbated. I may start seeing things again. I may start hearing things again. I may start *thinking* things again (e.g., *I'm the Messiah I'm the Antichrist I'm the motherfucking Virgin Mary*).

So she has me on lamotrigine that will act as the floor, and Zoloft, which will be my ceiling. That, and then Abilify with the clonazepam I'm already on to help with the nutty craziness that always ensues once I kind of lose my mind.

She then tells me that she wants me to try lithium. She says it will stabilize my moods. She says it will, *Help with your outlook.*

After reading the precautions on the label that they stick on the bag at the pharmacy, I find out that, basically, I can watch a head-on collision with limbs and heads and body parts flying every whichway without so much as a flinch or a sigh.

Sweet.

***

I wake up to the sound of the telephone.

The ringringring of the telephone wakes me and I sit up with a start. The air smells funny. Something is off. The air has a grainy quality to it. The sun seeps into the room and drenches my covers as I sit there trying to figure out what to do about the goddamn ringringring that won't stop.

At first I fear that it's work. I fear that it's Deets calling me to ask where I am, that it's eleven and where the hell am I, anyway? But it isn't even nine o'clock yet. Not even nine o'clock and the day's already gone to shit. Zapped to hell. Gone mad. With the hesitance of a frightened boy, I handle the receiver and pick the phone up, set it to my face, and say hello.

Hey, it's me …

Marianne. Little early.

It's almost nine, she says. *Why aren't you up?*

I am.

Something just happened. But I'm okay.

What happened?

I dunno.

What the hell, Marianne?

It happened a couple of minutes ago. Hold on—

There are screams of panic on the other end of the line. I'm stuck in my living room, helpless.

Holy shit, baby, she says. *Yeah, something just hit the building. Jesus, that's not good, is it?*

I whisper, *Get out of there.* Can't even speak. So scared.

Hold on.

The line gets muffled for a moment. She gets back on and she says she has to go. She has to go but will I come and see her later. She needs a drink; it's only nine and she needs a drink already. Would I mind?

Okay, I say. That was the last thing I said to her. Ever. (Sea of regret) *Okay*, I say to her. Then she died a few hours later. She and thousands like her. All. Dead. I remember the calmness in her voice when she said it, as if that kind of thing happened every Tuesday.

I remember the panic. The uncertainty. *What next*? I remember the debris and the ash and smoke and dust. I remember walking down Montague Street and seeing memos and emails floating in the air, lining the sidewalk and street. I stepped on a memo telling Paul Franklin about the meeting that afternoon on the eighty-seventh floor. There was a handwritten note asking Patricia if Robbie was still in school. Do you want to meet for lunch? Meet me downstairs at 12:00. See you soon.

Paul never made that meeting. Patricia never did have that lunch. And Robbie doesn't have a mother anymore. Just like that. Buried under tons of steel, they know their fate. It'll only get worse. They know that it's only a matter of time. I understand the feeling. Just like that, I remember the panic.

SEVEN: *Everyone Kind of Loses Interest*

I remember—wait …

Wait, now I—yes! Now I—

No.

Wait. Hold—

Okay—

My hand picks up the knife, the—wait—yes!—the thick sharppointy knife that sits on the table. The coffee table. I put it there *just in case*. Well, this is it. My hand picks up the knife and brings it to my neck. I feel the blade on my whiskers. Nudges the whiskers. Plays with the skin. The blade slides across the surface of my neck. Slides and slowly breaks the epidermis—

Wait, no—

Hold—

I'm at the séance in Union Square and everyone is singing "Imagine" and holding candles and *this* will stop me from aching inside, holding burning wax and listening to the words of a dead idealist. Whatever works, I suppose. I start to hold the candle close to my face, and I can feel the heat of it on my nose, the hairs inside my nose start to curl from the swelter.

All this singing for nothing, because Marianne is already dead. She's missing, but in my mind she's already dead and gone. Buried at least.

Yes!

No no no!

I'm sitting at a table in the back of the bar with my friends from work who aren't my friends at all and they're laughing and crying and making awkward jokes about Afghanis and Saudis and Bin Laden and whatall. I make a joke and someone says something about how his wife is dead. And says we shouldn't be laughing about this. And I start to cry and say that my girlfriend died, too, and it stings me so much that I can barely lift my eyes to the guy, who happens to be Pewterschmidt, and he looks at me and shakes his head and sees me crying and everyone starts to back away from me because I start mumbling and whispering and mutteringmutteringmuttering like my sister did way back when.

I start to say things that don't make any sense to anyone but me. I start saying things. I start to mumble things and I know that I'm too loud because after I say that my girlfriend died, someone makes another joke and Pewterschmidt glares at the guy and says, *Seriously, knock it off!*

And everyone kind of loses interest in drinks.

Pewterschmidt takes me home and we talk on the stoop of my building. His wife, Molly, died. Or, he thinks she's dead. Hasn't heard from her in a week. Can't be good. Wishes he'd treated her better. Last thing he said to her was, *Pick up some Cheerios on your way home,* he tells me. (Sea of regret)

Pewterschmidt starts to weep for his dead wife, and I realize I'm crying, too. He tells me that he didn't know I was even seeing anyone. He tells me Marianne was a good woman. I say she was. I say she was the best there ever was. That we had just gotten engaged. That she and I were planning a wedding for the next summer. He and I cry and cry and cry. He says he should go.

But it was nice to let it out, he says. *It's nice to get it all out,* he says. *Very cathartic,* he tells me. *Thanks.*

He walks—

No!

Hold the fucking—wait!

I'm sitting at the bar with Pewterschmidt and he looks over at me and says that they found her that afternoon. I say, *Jesus, I'm so sorry.*

Did they find Marianne?

No.

The bartender comes by with new drinks. Pewterschmidt asks me if I want to start a business together. If I want to start a little independent publishing house, he's always wanted to do that, do something unique like that; he'd call it Molly Press, he says, and then starts crying.

He asks me if I'm interested.

Nothing interests me anymore, I say to him. And for the first time in months, I realize I mean it.

He wipes his eyes and calls me a good man. I agree to go into business with him. When and where? I ask him. He says he's quitting Daniels & Webster next week. I say I will, too.

The next day, Deets is sitting quietly in his office when I walk in.

What? he asks without turning.

I'm giving my two weeks, sir,

Uh-huh, he says in a breath. Doesn't look at me. Won't even look at me.

You all right, sir? I ask for no reason.

I heard your fiancé was in the North Tower.

I think for a minute, then say, *Yes, she was.*

Sorry about that.

I look around the office nervously.

People are saying you lost your daughter, sir.

He says nothing. Just clears his throat. *I want a letter of resignation from you by the end of the day. And if that's all, you can go.* He motions for the door.

I walk out. I write the letter saying I'll quit. I give it to Deets and he says nothing. Just takes the paper without looking at me and sets it on his desk. Haze has hit the air of the office for the past two weeks. No one talks. No one seems to breathe. Plus side, no one stares at me anymore. Now that Marianne's dead, they know I'm real. I'm human. I am capable of love. So they talk to me now. They like me now.

Pewterschmidt shows me a real estate brochure at the end of the day and I see our future office. He tells me to call human resources to get my shit squared away. I call. My shit gets squared. I lose my insurance in a month.

A week later, Deets tells me that I'm free to leave. A week after that, Pewterschmidt and I apply for a loan under his name. Two days later, we're denied the loan. Three days after which I get a call from Pewterschmidt telling me that he's on the Bay Ridge Pier and he's going to do it! He swears to Holy Christ he's going to jump!

And he does before my cab gets there. So he's dead. He jumped into the Hudson Bay and let himself drown.

Yes.

Now I remember.

Yes. Now—

I hold the knife to my neck. It glides over my skin. I feel absolutely nothing. It would be nice to feel something. Jesus Christ! *Anything at all!* Then I feel the pinch as the nerves are spliced and the skin separates and I feel the blood trickletrickletrickle down my neck and soak into my shirt. Evil wetness. Yes! Now I know! I know! Yes! This is it! Yes! Deeper! Deeperdeeperdeeper! I'm gonna die!

Nothing I want more. And I know it now, and you might, too, one day, unless you already do, in which case, God help you.

I scream. I cry and wail and shout. A neighbor, annoyed by my noise, calls the cops. The cops come and knock on the door and must hear my screams because moments later I'm being dragged by the arms out of the apartment and into an ambulance that came from nowhere.

In the ambulance, they ask me some questions and I answer them as best I can with a gaping wound on my neck. I tell them about my fiancé. Marianne. And I tell them about the baby we were going to have. And all my future down the pot now.

My life is over, I tell them. I'm beside myself, weeping. My voice hoarse from screaming, raw, like nails scraping cement. *It's fucking over,* I say to them as the ambulance rolls away, lights flashing, siren blaring.

Keep still, they tell me.

You'll only make it worse, they say.

You're lucky you didn't hit an artery, someone says from behind me.

I close my eyes. I count to ten.

I think of Marianne.

***

The ambulance pulls up to the doors of a hospital in Brooklyn. The ambulance arrives at St. Michael the Hope and I get out on a stretcher. They take me in, they strap me down, they take me into the ER, and I'm there for a while. Then I'm upstairs. I'm in the nuthouse again and I'm there for a while. Again.

There.

Now I remember.

Yes!

Yes yes yes yes!

No—

Wait …

EIGHT: *The Unmistakable Aroma of Shit*

Once again, I was sent to triage and had to sit on a tabletop with my hands fastened to the bed and my feet tied together. And this supposed to make me *less* crazy? Being tied down like a fucking pig? Nurse Ratched came by and I told her I needed a drink.

If I get time, she says. She says, *If I get time.*

Well fuck you, too.

I was tied down for three hours, watching gaping chest wounds and bruisedup women get carted past me, when I realized I had to pee. I could feel the piss welling up inside my bladder, and oh God! did I have to go. Another half hour passed. I told whoever would listen to me that I had to use the bathroom right quick. Ten minutes later, I pissed all over myself.

Outstanding!

Unfortunately, not only was I sitting there with a gash in my neck, I was now covered waist down in cold urine.

Get me the fuck out of this bed! someone yelled, and after a few moments got himself free and then hit one of the doctors. He was drunk and I assumed he drank alone.

In hour eight, I figured out how I was going to kill Ken. But I wouldn't tell anyone. By hour eight and one quarter, I'd forgotten; I was just scared.

During hour eight and a half, a doctor wheeled me into a little room and stitched up my neck. It hurt worse than the knife did. I was wheeled back to triage.

I tried to sleep through hour nine, but trying to sleep in a triage unit is like trying to sleep in a triage unit. *This is hell,* kept replaying over and over and over in my mind. People were being carted in and out like bags of produce at a supermarket.

I thought of Marianne.

Finally, ten hours after I arrived—after ten hours of not moving and pissing myself silly—I was carted through a maze of plastered white walls that had a medicinal smell, like liquefied aspirin and cough syrup, vinegar and urine. The stink clung to them. I was just getting used to the sweet and sour odor when at the last door before the ward I smelled something different: the unmistakable aroma of shit.

***

Percy Shitstains squats against the creamcolored wall next to the employee bathroom and defecates in a neat little pile while no one pays any attention to him whatsoever. The man—short, bald, tubby—glances around like a deviant every couple of seconds, shitting like nobody's business. It really is a massive pile of shit. I'm not going to lie. Fucking cosmic. Suddenly there's a shout and a curse from one of the orderlies.

Hey! Fuck, Percy! Goddamn it, fuck! the orderly yells. *Brandy, you might want to see this!*

I'm laying on a gurney, still strapped down, my head turned to the side; I'm watching Shitstains; I'm watching him because I don't have a choice. It's either stare at him, or turn my head and stare at the boogers and other mucus-related goodies stuck to the wall on the other side of me.

I have to take a piss, I say softly.

Percy! What did we talk about yesterday? says Brandy, though for all, I know she could be Dusty Fucking Springfield.

Shitstains finishes his BM, and then stands over it, as if protecting his offspring.

I have to piss, I say a little louder. No one responds.

Guess I'll have to clean it up then, says Brandy. *Motherfucking psycho,* she says. Going to the nurses' station, she grabs paper towels and says, *Didn't sign up for this shit.*

I have to pee! I say louder now. No one responds and I realize that the person who wheeled me into the ward is gone. I have no idea where they went off to. But they're gone. I'm alone. And I will not piss myself again. Once in one night is plenty.

What are you in for? says a male voice—dark and husky; he sounds like Dad. I turn my head to see a big Indian-looking man who asks me again what I'm in for. I say suicide. He says, *Attempt?*

I give him a *no-I'mfuckingdead* look and say, *Yes, attempt.*

The man doesn't introduce himself. He just asks me if I feel dangerous to myself right now. I tell him I always feel dangerous to myself. He asks me if I feel like I'm going to hurt someone. I tell him no. I tell him I have to take a leak. He leaves and goes into the nurses' station and comes out with a bedpan.

Here you go, he says.

What the fuck is this?

What the fuck it look like?

I'm not going to pee in this.

Well, then I guess you're shit out of luck, ain't you?

Livid. Angry. Volatile. I glare at him. *Can I at least have some privacy?*

He rolls his eyes and shakes his head and wheels me into the employee bathroom and leaves me there next to the stalls and the urinal. He leaves without turning the light on. The room is almost completely dark, but not dark enough that I can't see the urine stains and the cumshots on the walls of the bathroom stall. There is a blue streak running down the side of the urinal from the urinal cake. It smells so pungent in here that I feel nauseated.

I shout out that I still can't move my arms to pee. No one responds and I try my best to position myself in such a way that I can pee into the bedpan while avoiding splashback or soakage.

After soiling much of my left leg and some of my right leg, I call that I'm done. I call and call and call and finally, after twenty minutes, they take me to a room, put a white sheet over me, and leave me there to sleep. This is the "safe room," used for people who are a threat to themselves or others. The "safe room" is a room with white walls and white ceiling and white floor. Very white. But in the dark, sometimes the whitest of the white seems fucking filthy. I can smell the odors of thousands of angry people in this room. The cover is barely covering me, and moments later, it falls to the floor. I fall asleep anyway.

***

I remember—

Um—

Nowait—

Yes, I remember the way Mother smelled when she walked with me to the school, me horrified at what was about to happen. Me petrified that someone would see me walking with my mother; my mommy coming to save me from the evil students and mean teacher who always scorns and ridicules me. I hate them all.

Mother smells of bread and potatoes and French perfume.

Yes, now here it—

Wait—

Yes, okay.

I had come home from school yesterday crying. I had come home crying because the people who taught me didn't care, and the students I was being taught with hated me for no other reason than I was Me. Me with a capital *M*.

Mike and Pat and Keith sit in front of me and at both sides. Front, right, left, the three of them constantly waiting for something to fire at me, something to hit me with. Anything they can get. Anything at all that they can use.

They aren't my friends who aren't my friends yet. They just aren't my friends. And when they *are* my friends who aren't my friends, it's even worse. Because then they're my friends. Who aren't my friends. Much worse.

Mike says, *Dolby, what are you doing?*

I'm doing my homework.

No, I mean, what are you reading there? (He takes the book from off my desk) *Jesus, what the fuck is this?* Of Mice and Men? *This looks gay.*

Who's gay? Pat asks, almost breathlessly, scrambling for something to make fun of me for. *What's gay?* he asks Mike, who's holding up the book I'd been reading.

Of Mice and Men, *that's what he's reading.*

Keith laughs but says nothing.

What about men, Dolby? You like men? says Pat, real snide-like.

No.

Do you like mice, Dolby? Into dogs and cats and shit? Mike whispers.

Shut up.

Keith scoffs and smirks and shakes his fucking stupid head. *Gay. Totally gay.*

Shut up.

Mike slaps the book again and it hits the floor. The teacher says nothing. Mike sneers, *You are so fucking gay, Dolby.*

Shut up! Shut up shut up shut up!

Then the mean teacher yells at me and tells me to stop talking, to stop making noise and do my homework. Mike throws the book in my face and smirks and turns to read the book he's doing his report on: *Batman: The Movie.*

I start to read again, but Keith keeps reaching over and swatting the book off my desk. I pick it up, and it gets swatted off. I pick it up, it gets swatted—

Yes!

Now I re—

Mother walks into the building with me in tow, and she goes to the offices and demands to speak to Principal Goldberg. *He's at a meeting, M*other is told.

Well, Mother says, *we'll wait.*

Shouldn't he be in class right now? asks the secretary, pointing in my direction.

Mother doesn't say a word until the principal comes out an hour later and demands to know why I am not in class. That I was marked delinquent that morning for not showing up. Mother tells him that she called me in as sick. The secretary tells the principal that she must have forgotten. This is all because I'm a goddamn Catholic instead of a fucking Lutheran. Mother is led into the office. The big office with big books on the wall.

We have a problem, says my mother.

You're right, we do, says the principal. And then, without letting Mother say what she needs to say, he scolds her. *Your son is disruptive in class. He doesn't do his homework. And, overall, he is a problem child. He's a slow learner. He doesn't follow directions, and he's failing many of his classes. Mrs. Dolby, your son is headed for disaster.*

He says all this with me four feet from his face. Right in front of me, he calls me these things. The principal goes on. My mother starts to cry and the principal doesn't offer her a tissue or anything. After the meeting, Mother tells me that I'll be going to the public school from now on.

We leave the school and I don't go back. Ever.

***

Fucksna-shitmonkeyfuck! So says Bailey, my new roommate. He says, *Fuckfuckfuck-cuntuntunt.* He looks at me. My eyes are now wide open and I stare at Bailey, all 250 pounds of him—all black and puffy— *Sorry, I have Tourette's—fuckuckuckshit!* he says. Then adds again, with the shame of a fool, "*Fuckmynoseshna! Fuckshitonyourface!*"

I nod. I'm scared shitless.

What brings you here? he asks me. Then adds, *Cocksmockock …*

Um … I start to say. But a nurse walks in, not Brandy—someone different—someone with three chins and two mongormous breasts and hair that looks pasted on in some spots. Her waxy scalp looking like a caramel apple. Drippy, gooey. I look at her and tell her that I need to bathe. That I feel like shit and I need to clean myself—get the piss off me.

She purses her lips like I just asked her to wax my balls. She shakes her head and says, *There's a bathroom right there, Mr. Dolby.*

Okay, I say and wander into to the closet of a bathroom and start the water, chilly at best. I pick up the wrapped soap, teenytiny elf soap, and start to unwrap it. My clothes now on the floor, I step into the stream of cold water and start washing. Using the teenytiny elf soap for lather, I wash my head and grimy body and pissdrenched legs. I get out and brush my teeth with the teenytiny toothbrush, rinse my mouth out with the teenytiny mouthwash. And I wonder if hospitals realize that when someone loses their mind, they don't lose body mass as well. Unless that's their thing. Cutcutcut.

I look at my wound. It's all slimy and pasty. Painful to wash. It's almost too painful to touch, but I do it anyway; it's nice to feel something in all this madness.

After washing and drying and getting some scrubs on, I poke my head out of the room and look down the hallway, the aroma of shit still hanging like fog in the air. The stench of stale urine is almost overpowering. Inching down the hallway, I pass the nurses' station and see that the nurses and orderlies are playing cards and eating pizza from Sargento's Pizza. I continue walking until I get to the day room where the patients are having dance therapy.

Dance therapy was invented by stupid people who thought to themselves:*You know what crazy people need most? Boy bands and a good ol' fashioned bump 'n grind!*

I eyed the crowd. One woman, who we'll call Wart, named thus due to the fifteen or so warts that covered each of her inhumanly long hands, was jumping like a mad person up and down to the pulsating bass of Britney Spears singing "Oops! I Did It Again." She was wearing a green turtleneck and a navy skirt with white socks and flip-flops. Her hair was matted against her face from the sweat. She was leaping into the air like a fucking moron.

There's Creepy Middle Aged Guy, rubbing his tool inconspicuously as he watches a young girl gyrate to the grooves.

There was Bailey.

There was Greasy (who, I could tell, went to these sessions simply to accumulate more grease to make him look like a basted turkey).

Jail Bait. Sixteen (maybe—*maybe* seventeen), getting a little *too* into therapy.

When a boy band comes on, Wart waddles over to me and asks me in a thick Polish accent, *You want girlfriend?*

No. Not really, I mutter nervously. She proceeds to grab my crotch.

You get girlfriend any time, she whispers, and lets go.

Big Beefy Guy. Big. Beefy. He gets out of his room, walks the length of the hallway.

That girl just grabbed my balls, I tell him.

Great, she'll stop grabbing mine, he says.

***

After therapy, Wart tried to grab my nuts again and I swatted her hand away, and then went to wash, trying to scrub the fungus off. Bailey was masturbating when I entered the room. I just went into the bathroom like I didn't notice. I think he appreciated that, because when I got out of the bathroom, he was curled up in a ball, sleeping.

***

I was not allowed to smoke. I was not allowed to read. I was not allowed to eat anything but the hospital approved menu. I was not allowed to watch TV unless it was watched during the designated "TV time," every night at 8:00. I was not allowed to open windows, wear belts, wear shoelaces, use sharp silverware, shave, go near curtains, listen to music (except at dance therapy, of course), go near female patients unless we were in group meetings (big fucking loss). I couldn't use the phone unless I cleared it with an assistant or an orderly. I couldn't have visitors and I couldn't write letters.

The place was a Kafka novel.

That night at group session, Wart was staring at my unit the whole time and it was so creepy that I had to leave the meeting and go to bed. I woke up at 2:00 in the morning to the sounds of masturbation.

I didn't sleep for the rest of the night.

I thought of Marianne.

NINE: *You Get Better, All Right?*

I wake up at eight in the morning thinking I'm at home in bed with Marianne next to me. Turning over, I smile big and say hello to my goddamn pillow. She's dead. I keep forgetting. It's amazing what the mind chooses to forget.

I eat breakfast and swallow down my yellow fluff (eggs) and leather straps (bacon), swill down the Sunny Delight, and try to finish the coffee they gave me that so obviously came from an AA meeting down the street. I can seriously taste the cigarette butts. After food, I ask an orderly named Julian if I can use the phone to call my doctor.

No. Absolutely not.

Why?

Hospital policy. No phones. Not until the doctor clears it.

But I haven't seen my doctor.

No phone then.

But I need to call my doctor to let her know what happened.

No phone, Dolby.

Wait! Listen to me. I have to call my doctor, tell her that I'm here, while I'm on the phone with her, I'll have her clear whatever you need cleared! But I can't call her to get clearance if I can't use the phone!

No. Phone. Dolby. Not until your doctor sees you. We're going to call her—

What do you mean 'We are going *to call her?'*

I mean that we will call her.

You haven't called her yet?

No. We will, though.

I've been here for, like, two days now!

Look, Dolby, listen to me good: You will not use that goddamn telephone. You will not! Period!

Can I write her a letter?

Sure.

Great. I'll do that.

Very good.

You have a stamp I could use?

Julian glares at me and shakes his head. *We aren't going to give you a stamp. You provide your own stamps. Okay?*

I don't have stamps. I don't carry them around with me.

Then I guess you're shit out of luck, Dolby! Now go to group therapy and get the hell off my back.

Where can I get stamps? I ask him.

Have someone bring you some, I dunno.

No one knows I'm here!

Then you're fucked. Go to therapy. Now!

I go to therapy. Fucking A.

***

Later that afternoon, the hospital apparently got a call across to my doctor, because she was on the phone when I got up from my midafternoon nap.

Hello? I say to her, hoping she won't yell at me for what I did. Although I know she won't, I know she'll want to.

Hi. What the hell is going on?

I'm in the hospital.

Where?

St. Michael the Hope.

103

Well, at least you aren't at Belleview.

Perchance to dream.

You didn't call me. Damn it, why didn't you call me?

I look around the hallway, making certain no one can hear me.

I was too scared.

She sighs. She sighs again.

You're going to be seeing a doctor there who I've never heard of. I know you won't be able to see me, because I'm with First Presbyterian. Bureaucracy at work. St. Michael the Hope won't have me coming in to treat you. So you follow whatever this new doctor tells you. Okay?

Okay.

You need to call me next time something like that happens.

Okay.

Okay?

Okay.

She sighs again. *Okay, call me tomorrow after you talk to your new doctor.*

Okay. But I'm having trouble using the phones.

You pick up the receiver and push the buttons.

I try to laugh. I can't. We say our goodbyes and I hang up the phone.

***

My doctor clears me, so I can use the phone, so I call my mother and she's not there, so I hang up. Then I go for my late afternoon nap.

I have a strange dream.

***

I get up and call my mother again. I get the answering machine. *Leave a message at the tone*, whatnot. I do. I tell Mother that I'm in the nut house again, that I should be out shortly. And that some guy was shitting on the floor a day or two ago. No biggie. As I hang up, the line comes to life and a male's voice says, *Hello? Is that you, buddy?*

Donald. Thank my sweet Lord and savior Thom Yorke.

Yeah, uh, it's me.

Where are you? The fucking world is caving in over here!

What do you mean?

Dad had a stroke. Mom's nuts with worry. You gotta get up here.

How's Leigh?

She's fine. Get out and get up here.

I can't. It's not that easy. You know that.

The line is quiet. Suddenly, Leigh takes over—Leigh is his wife—and she wants to know how I am. What's the deal? What the fuck?

I tell her about Percy Shitstains. I tell her about Bailey. About this and that and the other. And she says to me, she says, *You get better, all right?*

And I feel the need to remind her that my arm isn't broken and I don't have the goddamn flu. I'm nucking futs over here and it doesn't work that way!

Right. 'Kay. Talk to you soon. She almost moans the words. Like me getting out of a fucking mental hospital after slicing up my neck should be as easy as walking out of a shitty movie half-way through.

I'll tell Dad you say hi, okay?

I tell her okay, that she should give him a big hug for me. Tell him I love him. Whatever.

***

These were my new instructions:

Son, you will take two hundred milligrams of lamotrigine—three milligrams of Rispirdal—three hundred milligrams of lithium—two hundred of welbutrin—and thirty milligrams of Abilify. So says my new doctor. He goes on These will give you a floor and a ceiling in terms of moods, and the Abilify and Rispirdal will dull the psychosis—make it more manageable. Now, as you may already know, he says, stroking his beard. *You need to take medication to stabilize your symptoms. I believe you suffer from what's known as "schizo-affective disorder."*

And that is?

Ho, ho, ho, he says like Father-fucking-Christmas. *It's a combination of many things, but what we're looking at here is schizophrenia and bi-polar disorder. You have psychosis, of that I'm sure. But you have a lot of everything.*

Oh. Nice. Very nice. Thanks for the good news. *What are some of the symptoms?*

Well, let's see, he says, looking down at his notes and scratching his fuzzy chin. *Well, okay. One thing is that you'll see things. Maybe a bug or mice crawling across the floor. Another thing would be that you have irrational thoughts. Maybe that people are watching you, talking about you, thinking about you. You'll think people are out to get you, or that they can read your mind and—right, there is one major thing that you need to be aware of.*

Yeah?

If you stop taking your medication for any length of time, however short, and start becoming psychotic, you will *feel the effects immediately. It'll start small. You'll think you lost your keys or your wallet and check and recheck because you don't recall checking. Or you'll, say, do the dishes and you'll do the same dish over and over again because you can't seem to get all the dirt off. You'll put the dish back, then take it out to wash it again because you're* sure *you didn't clean it. Or you'll start thinking the cats—you have cats?* I shake my head. *You'll start thinking the cats are talking to you.*

Andrew P. H. Clyde

I don't have cats.

It's like I'm not even here. Jesus Christ. He goes on, *And your thoughts. You need to be aware of what's going on in your head. You're thought processes will be skewed to say the least. Words will make so sense. You'll lose your train of thought. Your mind will—well, it won't be good.*

Okay.

When you get bad—and I mean, really bad, *you'll get what in layman's terms are "cyclical thoughts." It's severe psychosis. Your mind is so confused that it turns in circles. Say you're severely psychotic—something has triggered a psychotic reaction, something traumatic or whatever—you'll begin having cyclical thoughts.*

Again. Good news for me. I not going to lie. I feel like shitting my fucking pants.

You'll be at point A, then go to the logical point B, then point C, then D, then you'll go back to C, then B, then back to A. It's like that ride at Coney Island, what's it called?

The teacups?

Like that one ride where you go in circles. What's it called?

The teacups?

That one ride. What's it—whatever. Anyway, you need to be taking your new meds consistently. If you don't, the delusions come back, the cyclical thinking occurs, the—

I stop him. *Wait. What delusions?*

108

Like I'm not even in the fucking room. *Now, what you may not know is that if you stop taking your pills, cold turkey or otherwise, the side effects of withdrawal will be—to put it mildly—unbearable.*

Yeah, I say. *You mentioned.*

It's going to get bad. A kind of torture. Everything will be intensified, the paranoia, the psychosis, the depression, the mania, everything.

I love pep talks. I ask him why he's changing my meds around. *The other meds I was on seemed to work fine, just fine.*

Well, those meds got you in here and you have your doctor to thank for that.

She didn't cut my throat. I did.

He clucked his tongue and shook his head. *Mr. Dolby, I think you should trust me. I'm a doctor; I know what I'm doing.*

I'm assuming my other doctor knew what she was doing and I ended up in here. If I can't trust her judgment, what makes you think I can trust yours?

The smile was gone. *Mr. Dolby. You are here to get well. Now I want to help you. Do you want to get better?*

(No, I want to stay in this hole for the rest of my natural life, you dumb fuck.) *Yes,* I tell him. *Yes,* I say again.

Then trust me.

***

The summer is spent alone—no, wait, no—

The whole summer is only me and Donald—fuck—

School starts in two weeks and I have no friends and—

No, wait—

I remember—

Yes! I remember now, I—

The school looms like a mountain on the horizon at the end of Clinton Street, a gianthugemassive mountain that I now have to climb, have to overcome, and I have to do it without help from anyone, least of all God, whom the principal told Mother would not be in the new school, that God was absent from public schools. My world is so small, my feet too teenytiny to walk up the mountain. I am small and girlish. I am tender and fresh. I am not ready to be alone, without help—least of all from God—and I want my mother as I step through the doors. Donald is at the high school. I'm starting seventh grade and that means I'm in junior high, which means I have *hours* instead of *classes.*

I have math first hour.

I have P.E. second hour.

Study hall third, lunch is open campus—I can go anywhere in town—the rest of the hours are social studies, careers, science, English, and art.

I hate all the classes because I'm no good in any of them. But at least the teachers are nice about it. Not like the fucking Lutherans.

You certainly do try, one tells me.

You must have spent a lot of time on this, says another.

All you can do is your best, says Mrs. Pierce. I like Mrs. Pierce. Everyone likes Mrs. Pierce. She's beautiful and I'm falling in love with her.

You have beautiful penmanship, she says and smiles at me. I look at her chest the whole time, her loveliness showing just a bit out of the neckline of her shirt. I stare and stare and then feel weird and funny in my privates. Then my—

No! No! Now I—

Yes!

The girl!

She's there in the back of the room, and no one sees her but me. Her name is Mary Ann McCormack. "Marianne," she likes to spell it. And I can't talk to her because if she knows I like her, she may hate me. I can't tell her that I like her because then she'll know I like her. That wouldn't be good, would it?

So I talk to her. But she doesn't say much. But I keep trying. And trying and trying and trying until she finally says, *You're cute.*

And I feel my privates swelling again, and I have to cover them with an English book. She doesn't seem to notice. She wants to know where I live, and I tell her I live on Walnut Street. She says she lives on North Main, and would I like to walk her home?

Could you walk me home? she asks.

I hold the book against my lap and nod until she smiles and walks away. I calm down enough to walk to final hour. After which we walk home and I fall in love with Mary Ann. M-A-R-I-A-N-N-E, she spells it …

That night, I think of Mary Ann.

TEN: *I Am the Moon*

I spoke with Bailey about his life for a while and afterwards I decided that I'd had about enough Life for one lifetime. Life with a capital *L*.

Sometimes I get the impression that if Life were any better, it would still completely suck. He was abandoned by his standup, just plain kickass parents in a Brooklyn pizza shop called Tribiano's on Fifteenth Street near Prospect Park. The owner found him sitting in the bathroom, Bailey covered in his own filth. Cleaned up, he was taken to Mother Mary's Home for Children. He stayed there for ten years, making friends, making enemies, until a nice, young, white couple from Manhattan adopted him—such nice white folk, adopting a poor black child (here's your medal)—and abandoned him at Jones' Beach four months later. (About that medal)

The parents were never found. Why? Because Bailey didn't know where they lived. Why? Because Bailey couldn't read. He didn't know what street they lived on.

He couldn't take anyone there because Manhattan is a labyrinth of buildings and blocks and a tenyearold won't be able to find his way back home to save his life even if he could read. He had Tourette's, Bailey says to me.

They—lickmyassfuck—abandoned me because I was different—pissinmyshit!

He went back to the home until he was seventeen and then ran away, became a truck driver, got fired, became a fisherman—fired—a janitor at a school in the Bronx, fired because the kids were picking up words like *fuckcockshitmonkey*, and the like. Fired fired fired, the story of our lives.

Now he lives off government checks in Queens. Some great life the mentally ill have, living on social security. He certainly did win the fucking jackpot on that one. He gets a good $750 a month for living in pure, unadulterated, living, bleeding, wish-he-was-dead hell every day and night from now into perpetuity. Good stuff. Totally worth the seven-fifty a month. Yes indeed, we disabled mentally ill sure are the lucky ones, aren't we?

I'm not mad, though, he says, and I want to ask him why. I want to tell him that he should be mad. That I would be mad. That anyone would be mad and angry and hating the world!

But instead I just nod and say, *Wow.*

It was about nine, almost time to stare at the ceiling until dawn, so I got into bed and watched some leaves blow around my windowsill. I tried to sleep. I couldn't.

I thought of Marianne.

***

I was now allowed to smoke. I had to go outside to the courtyard. It was a fourteen-by-twenty area in the middle of the hospital grounds that looked a lot like the people who designed the place said, *In eighty years smoking won't be allowed anywhere in New York, so let's give those sorry sons of bitches a little nook where they can smoke to their hearts' content for twenty minutes every day.*

I have a friend who was into heroin. She tells me that if she didn't get a hit every day she went ape. She tells me that once she was at her desk at work when she got a hankering for some smack and ran off to the bathroom to give herself mercy right then. That's how bad she needed her fix.

I am addicted to nicotine and that's about it. Ken will tell you otherwise, but smokes are all I need and to tell me that I can have all the cigarettes my body needs for the next twenty-four hours in twenty minutes in a little courtyard is like telling my friend that she could shoot up all she wants one day a year and that's all the shit she can pour into her veins. Regardless, I'm outside smoking my third cigarette in ten minutes when Jail Bait walks up to me and asks if I want a blow job.

I'll give you one, she says. *Not here, but later, in the bathroom.* (Molested as a child)

That's okay, I tell her. *Really.*

Fine, faggot. Fuck you then, she says, and walks over to Beefy Guy and must ask him the same question because he grins an evil grin and nods his head. Glances at me and smiles and gives me the universal sign for a "hand job." He takes a puff of his cigarette and gazes at the outside world beyond the fence.

***

Going back inside, Bailey tells me that my mother called. So I call her back and she starts to cry.

What did I do? What did I do to you to make you like this?

I don't know what to tell her. *Bad genes, I guess,* I say, and immediately wish I hadn't. A wail is heard on the other end of the line. *Jesus, Mom, you didn't* do *anything. It's just the way it is. There's nothing we did to do it and there's nothing we can do to undo it.*

Well, shucks, that's just ducky! she hisses, as if talking to someone in authority. Apparently God is standing in the room with her.

Mom.

Yes, sugar?

Can you get me out?

I called to tell you that I got a letter in the mail saying your insurance runs out next week. Ask your doctor if you can be transferred up to Connecticut—maybe here to Hartford. UConn Medical Center. My insurance may cover you up here. There are special cases where certain people, in certain situations, can—well, this is one of those special cases and I think you can be put on my insurance until we can get yours figured out.

Mom. I'm thirty. How the hell am I going to be put on your insurance? It doesn't work that way.

Then we'll get you on Medicare or something! We'll figure it out. Just ask your doctor if you can be transferred.

I'll ask.

She takes a deep breath and sighs. *You heard about your father?* She starts crying again.

Yes. Will he be all right? I mean, is everything going to be okay?

You know when you're a kid and you simply want your mother to make it all better, to make the world a great and lovely place, and to know that it's all going to be all right?

I don't know, she says, and I'm left with such doubt and confusion that I hang up on her.

***

In my new doctor's office, I ask him if I can be transferred on account of my insurance running out.

Not if you're a threat to yourself. No.

Okay. I'm not a threat. Now, can I go? I can possibly be covered under my mother's insurance if I go to Connecticut.

That's where I'm from. I can be claimed as a dependent or get Medicare or—

I'm sorry, he says.

Well, then can I leave? I mean, I can't afford the three-thousand dollar a day tab for staying in this Psycho Hilton.

You can't leave if you're a threat to yourself.

Well, I say, *I think I would know if I'm a threat. I have to leave here now because come next week I can't pay for it!*

He tells me that he needs a few more days to see if I'm really okay. I ask him, since he makes the big bucks, if he can pay for my stay. He asks me to leave.

***

That night, I walked around the ward on my way to nowhere. I just walked the halls thinking. Mainly about Dad and the way he always made me feel smart and good and capable of doing anything. I thought of the stroke. I thought of him pissing himself in his hospital bed. I thought of the parallels between Dad and me. Pissing in a bedpan, having his ass wiped by a man or woman who'd rather be doing any number of things: write a book, have a child, *not* wipe shit out of someone's ass-crack.

I see Beefy Guy step out of the employee bathroom with a big, satisfied smile on his face, relief washed over him. It looks like he just had the best orgasm of his life. Then Jail Bait steps out, looking hurt and degraded.

I go to the nurses' station and ask for a cup of juice. Surprise of surprises, the juice cups they give you are just that: cups—as in one cup sour cream—and I take my pills along with an Ambian to help me sleep. I haven't been sleeping and I've been taking the Ambian for three nights now, and I still can't sleep. I've been told the doctor knows what he's doing.

The doctor knows what he's doing. You can't sleep? Here's your pill.

But I'm taking the pill and I'm still not sleeping. Which leads me to believe the doctor doesn't quite know exactly what the fuck he's—

Just take the pill, Mister Dolby!

I go to bed. Bailey is already there, and for the first time since coming here to the Happy House, I'm genuinely scared. Petrified. Sick.

I start to whimper.

You okay, man? he asks.

I have a cold. I am not going to cry in front of this freak. *I just have a cold. I'm fine.*

***

It was around this time that I knew for certain I didn't need to be in the nut house. I wasn't crazy. I was sane as shit. They're all nuts as fuck around here.

***

119

Mom called again the next morning and said that Dad had another stroke the night before. That there wasn't much time now. I needed to come home.

Going to my appointment with my new doctor, I asked if I could be transferred yet.

No, he says.

Well, can I at least leave the hospital for a day or two to see him?

No, Not in this condition.

Listen, my father is really ill and I need to see him. He may die!

Then he says in his grandfatherly voice, *Mr. Dolby, I cannot with a clear conscience let you out of here if I think you will be a threat to yourself or others.* He says this like he was reading it off of a note card. *I think your dear old father would appreciate that.* (Like he's old fucking chums with my dad)

I feel like saying, *Well, with all due respect, I think that me seeing my father before he dies takes precedence over what you think he would want. I know my father pretty damn well.* I want to shout, *And I think I know that he'd like to see me before he is not physically able to see me again.*

My new doctor leans towards me. I want to take a bite right out of that fucking beak of his. *Mr. Dolby. Do you trust me?*

And I'm dying to scream, *Like I trust a fucking terrorist, and don't call me that!* But instead I mutter, *Yes.*

Good, he says, rubbing his white, bushy chin. *Very good. Then let me tell you this: your father will be around when you get out of St. Michael's, and he'll be happy to see you then. All right? Have fun at dance therapy!*

My father died that night.

***

I found out the next day. My mother called at nine in the morning just as I was finishing my third juice cup. *He's gone.* She was weeping. I wanted to kill my new doctor. *He went to sleep while I was reading to him and he died after I got home.*

What where you reading him? Wart was walking towards me.

What? Mother asked, all incredulous-like, as if I just asked if I could see her boobs when I got out.

I was distracted. *What were you reading to him?*

She told me, but by then I wasn't paying any attention to her. Wart was stroking her left breast and licking her lips. I wanted to retch. *Mom, listen. I'll take care of this. I'm sure I can go to the funeral.*

Mom started to cry again. Poor woman, she'd never really loved anyone other than Dad. Dexter included. She loved Dex like a woman loves a pretty antique necklace. I knew she was thinking of Dad. So was I. I loved him so much. I wished I could be him. I wished I was him. I always did. When I was a kid, I wanted to be my dad.

Have arms like him so I could hold myself when I was alone and scared and afraid of Me.

You miss him, Mom?

She didn't say anything. Just whimpered. I whimpered. We both fucking whimpered.

She thought of Dad. I knew she thought of him.

I thought of Marianne.

Hazel eyed.

Pert nosed.

Thick lipped, soft voiced, dough breasted, warm haired, fresh skinned, standing, running, stopping, smiling, turning, looking down, looking up, smiling, watching, looking, inviting, eyeing, grinning, playful cheery sad sweet randy prude cautious fragile cold hot light dark day night black white itchy moody angry touchy feely brilliant mad distant close lovely dour laughing crying slapping swatting breathless dancing weeping scratching pressing holding kissing fleshsweatspitunion Mineminemineminemine …

She smelled like Dove face lotion and daffodils. Her eyes were so awfully blue. Tilted smile. A wide, toothy, tilted smile. When she laughed, you *knew* she was laughing. The whole world laughed when she did. Marianne made fantastic pancakes. She would make a burnt batch and say they were for her, then give me the best ones. Her hair was so blonde and long and beautiful. She always said that her hair didn't look professional. Her glorious hair. Held back in a ponytail. She always said she never felt pretty. But I thought she was lovely. And I never told her. She would say things like, *I love you,* and she would mean it. Not just mean it. But *mean* it. She said she loved me for Me—Me with a capital *M*. I never told her that I loved her voice. I never told her that the sound of her breathing made me smile. And she's gone. And she's never coming back. And I never told her why, or how, or if, or when. I never told her anything and she'll never know. Ever. (Sea of regret)

I thought of Marianne.

***

In tenth grade, Mike and Pat and Keith come to the public school from the fucking Lutheran school and they see me with some friends, my public school friends, and they have no friends because there are only twenty-three kids in the ninth grade class from St. Martin's, and they have no friends when they come to the high school, so they start hanging out with me and my friends, and then my friends are their friends, and then I get the crazies and then I'm only Mike and Pat and Keith's friend, but only because I have a mother who's never home and a father who doesn't live there, so they can smoke and drink and such at my house. And they do. So I get to hang out with them. And I do, but they don't like me.

And I don't like them. But I'm so lonely. I'm so starved for friendship. I need them.

So they come over to my white-washed house and they sit on the back porch watching the summer sun—large coin—setting over the houses lining Walnut Street. They sit there and smoke marijuana and drink my mother's lite beer. When Mom comes home, she's going to ask where her beer went, and I'll say I drank it, even though I don't like beer and she knows it. I do it because if Mom knew Mike and Pat and Keith were stealing her beer and doing drugs on her porch watching the quarter in the sky sink down into the river, she'd ban them. Alone again. Naturally.

So I protect them, and Mom has to ground me even though I don't even drink.

When I do start to drink, Mom won't let me out of the house ever. So I sneak out. Late at night, I sneak out and find my friends who aren't my friends, and we go and drink and smoke and meet girls down at the golf course, the moon shining lonely light down on us from the sky.

And I think to myself, *The moon must be so lonely. So all alone up there in the dark.*

And I love the moon in that instant. When I get the crazies, at night, when it usually happens, my friends who aren't my friends sometimes leave me alone at the golf course. I never get a make-out partner; I just supply my friends who aren't my friends with a place to sleep when I'm not grounded. The only reason they let me tag along is because I steal cigarettes from the supermarket down the street. I steal cartons of cigarettes and bring them along, namely because my friends who aren't my friends won't do it themselves.

But when we sneak out, it's only their girlfriends who come. And if there is another girl who comes, she never wants to be with me. I have to be alone for two or three hours, just me and the moon, and I smoke cigarettes and drink my mother's lite beer even though I hate it, and wish the moon and I could be friends if only for one night. Because I am the moon.

At night when I go to bed, I ask God to either kill me or give me a friend. That's when he reminds me of Mary Ann, the girl from the back of the class. She was my friend in junior high school, but stopped being my friend when Mike and Pat and Keith came along. Because she wasn't as cool as they were, apparently. The coolest people on Earth being fucking Lutherans, apparently.

So when we sneak out the next Friday and I'm alone on the grass, I think of Mary Ann. Marianne. And I wish she was there with me.

ELEVEN: *What the Hell Is so Heartbreakingly Funny …*

My new doctor can barely move when I tell him that my dad's dead. It's like he's frozen in carbonite. Like Han Fucking Solo. Goddamn it, I hate this man.

We all have to go sometime, he says to me. He actually says this to me!

I would have liked to have seen him.

I'm sure you certainly would have, but you were in here getting better. You have to understand that it was in your best interest to remain under supervision.

I look at him.

You have to trust me, Mister Dolby.

I glare. Really glare at the bastard.

Mister Dolby. Do you trust me?

Fuck you, I say, and walk out of the room.

***

I call Dr. Sprat and start crying instantly. She listens as I talk about my dad, and I don't give a good goddamn if people see me.

We'll work on this, she says.

Okay.

I'm going to make some calls tomorrow. We'll see if we can get you home before the week is up. I have a feeling the hospital is doing more harm than good.

We make idle chit-chat until she asks me what meds I'm on. I tell her and she says, *That's interesting. Good. How's therapy going?*

I can dance a mean Charleston, I say, and we hang up.

***

That night I thought a lot.

I thought about my dad. I thought about Ken and how much I wanted to hurt—really, truly hurt him. I thought about Shitstains and his shenanigans on the floor. I thought about me and my life and how fucked up everything was getting. I thought about Bailey and how fucked up his life already was. I thought about how alone I was. I thought about going to Patriots games with my father when I was a kid. I thought about the hotdogs at Fenway Park. I thought about Christmas.

I was happy then.

Yes—

Opening presents with the tree all pretty and such. I thought about my brother and dead sister and how they both acted like they loved the things I'd gotten them even if they really didn't. How they'd open them every year and laugh and hug me. I thought of how they never did that anymore and will never do that again. I thought about my sister's funeral when I was eight years old and how we were now going to do it all over again.

I thought about Marianne. The sounds of Bailey masturbating muted, somewhat, the sounds of my sobbing. I thought and thought and thought.

And there she was.

I thought about Marianne.

***

My next visit with my new doctor is my last.

I walk into the office and glance out the window—a window facing a wall with twenty other windows reflecting our wall. I look outside and see a small, battered Snickers wrapper floating in the air, being tossed around by the wind. Snickers satisfies you.

So, we were talking yesterday about your father, he says, breezing right by the fact that his brilliant diagnosis kept me from seeing my dad before he died.

I'm going to the funeral, I tell him.

He nods.

I'm going to the funeral and there's nothing your fucking diagnosis or medical opinion is going to do to stop that.

He nods again. *Yes, I figured as much.*

I felt like beating the man with the many diplomas that lined the office walls.

You kept me from seeing my dad, I hiss through tears that are dying to show themselves, to spurt from my eyes and fall to the floor. But I won't cry in front of this man. He doesn't deserve to know how much my dad meant to me. He doesn't deserve it! He doesn't get to know how I ache inside just thinking about the way he'd tell me he knew I'd amount to something. How he'd hold me when I cried. How he was my best friend and how my whole body just wants to cry out and scream, *Daddy, don't go! Please don't go and don't leave me here with these crazy people!* He doesn't get to know how much I love my dad, and how desperately I'm going to miss the everloving hell out of him. I can see his green eyes now, even as I glare at the man who made me miss Dad's last words. Now Dad will never know that he was my god on Earth. He'll never get to know that. This doctor raped me of my last words, and I'll never, ever forgive him for that.

I'm leaving. I'm going and you and your fucking diagnosis won't keep me from the funeral or being with my mother and brother when they need me. Threat or not. He wanted to see me.

He wouldn't have wanted to see you like this, I can assure you.

I disagree.

And that's all I say. I stare at the doctor and he looks away, and he knows that once I leave I'm not coming back—to this hospital, at least.

He pulls open his desk drawer and pulls out a pad of prescriptions. After writing five out, he hands them to me. *Take these at least. And take them religiously. Please.*

I grab them and walk out. I didn't thank him. My dad was still dead.

***

I smoke my first joint on my mom's porch when I'm seventeen and I almost lose my fucking mind, and all in front of Mike and Pat and Keith, who don't have a fucking clue what to do. They just sit there and gawk at me, their mouths wide open, as if goading someone who's on medication to smoke dope and then that person getting a psychotic reaction was something they weren't quite ready to take responsibility for. Like it's a total fucking surprise that I'd lose my goddamn mind.

God, you are such a buzzkill, Dolby, Pat says.

Never again, says Mike, and they start to get up.

But I tell them I'll do it, just this once I'll do it, just sit down, please, just don't go. So I put the butt to my lips and take a big inhalation and instantly feel my stomach turn. I hold it inside me as the other guys stare and smile and nod their big fucking Lutheran heads, very satisfied with themselves. And then my stomach turns and my eyes water and I exhale. I feel at first like there's cake batter in my head, goopy and drippydrippydrippy, coming out my ears and—

Fuck me—

Yes! This is the big—

And I fall back onto one of the chairs and it falls over and I fall to the floor. Nothing better than a high, let me tell you!

The guys laugh at me until I shout, *I'm dying!*

I'm dying I'm dying I'm dying I'm dying, oh my God! I'm going to die!

I scream and scream and scream as the world starts to fade in and out and in and out and the guys start flipping out saying, *Oh, shit! Oh, fucking God! What the fuck—*

I'm dying! I scream.

I scream and scream and scream.

I see the world come in and out of focus: tree lawnmower grass bush cat wind breeze car horn breeze wind cat bush grass lawnmower tree lawnmower grass bush cat wind breeze car horn breeze wind cat bush grass cat wind breeze car horn breeze cat lawnmowertreelawnm owergrassbushcatwindcarhornbreezewindcatbushgrass— *Oh my God! I'm dying dying dying dying dying dying!*

Shit, what the fuck? someone says like a frightened child.

Do we leave him? someone says like an irritated brother.

Let's just go, someone says like a weary mother.

This is my family. My friends who aren't my friends are my fucking family. I hate them so much. I just want them all to fall off the face of the fucking Earth. But they won't. And I won't let them. Because I need them. Because I'm so lonely that at nights I pretend I'm making love to someone. That someone is my pillow. That's how starved I am for contact with people. And when they get up to leave, I feel lost and scared and deserted as the sky swirls and the grass talks and the rocks and birds and trees scream at me and they're leaving and I want them to help me! Fuck you guys, why won't you help me? Stay with me? Make me feel better, make me feel safe like friends should? Why won't you treat me like a living breathing aching lost petrified loony pathetic human being? Don't go! Don't go! Don't leave me with the frowning sun and the laughing trees and monstrous ogres looming behind the bushes and the cats and mice and birds and bees all howling and no, no, no, no no no no no, don't leave me!

My head feels heavy and I feel my heart stop. My head crying bloodymurder bloodymurder and the like as no—Wait!

Yes!

And the wind and the bush and the cat and the lawnmower and yes yes yes! All of it leads to something!

Yes! No! Oh, please, God in heaven, no!

Not this!

Wait—

All of it leads to the time when I was a kid and there was the backs of penguins like drippydrippy wax, and the water of the tank and the spiders and ohGodno! My sister gone, yes—

No!

And she's at the house of cheese and then I go to class and teacherteacher says I'm—

And my friends hate me and I leave school and I spend the summer alone and I meet a girl and I get a boner and I walk her home and I hang out with new friends and I become friends with my friends who aren't my friends and I steal cigarettes and I sneak out and drink lite beer and smoke pot on the porch and—*OhmyGodI'mdying*—tree lawnmower grass bush cat wind breeze car horn breeze wind cat bush grass lawnmower tree lawnmower grass bush cat wind breeze car horn breeze wind cat bush grass cat wind breeze car horn breeze cat lawnmowergrassbus hcatwindcarhorn—

Fuck no!

Breezewindcatbushgrass—*Oh my God! I'm dying dying dying dying dying dying!*

And I go round and round and sit on the porch and dig a trowel blade into my arm and don't feel anything; just dig with the dull blade of a trowel and I'm remembering things that come round and round and soon Mother comes home and she screams and calls my doctor and we take a ride and—

Yes!

Wait.

***

I don't know what happened, but when I wake at 2:00 in the morning, Bailey is sobbing. I almost ask him what's wrong, but don't. I don't have to.

You awake, man? he whispers.

Yeah.

Then he tells me that Jail Bait tried to hang herself in the girl's bathroom with a shower curtain. He tells me that she's bleeding from the mouth and her privates are all fucked up. And she blames him. Bailey.

Bailey's being blamed because he's big and he's black. No. Not the dumbass jock. Not Beefy Guy. Bailey's the best damn scapegoat the ward has to offer.

They all think I did it. It's her word against mine. Fuckuckuck—

They can't—

I don't finish. I don't have to. He gets up and leaves the room and I gradually fall back sleep.

***

The next day I'm given leave papers and sign the dotted line. I get to go home for the weekend. My mother will be by tomorrow morning to sign me out.

Art therapy goes well. Wart isn't there and that's a relief. I draw a picture of my dad and me raking leaves. It's juvenile, but who the fuck cares. I loved him.

After lunch, me and about twelve others go outside for twenty minutes to smoke. I mooch a cigarette from Beefy, who confides in me that he got laid last night. He describes in painful detail how he fucked and left the mysterious lady in question. He says it's just his luck there's Bailey. Then stops suddenly.

Then, as if talking about a completely different incident, and a completely different person, and as if I'm a complete fucking idiot who can't put two and two together, he says, "*She's fucking crazy! Imagine, a shower curtain. That goddamn nigger freak is in for a world of trouble!*

He shakes his jock head and laughs his jock laugh, smiles that fucking jock smile that gets people like him anything they want.

Serves her right, though, he says.

It wasn't really Bailey who fucked her up, though, right? I mean, it wasn't him. He gives me a strange look. I go on. *Because I heard that everyone in this unit is gay.*

He scoffs. *Speak for yourself, faggot. I got me the best ass of my life just last night.*

He keeps talking. Mainly about Jail Bait's privates, putting two and two together for me. Thank God, my brain was hurting. Bailey had been through enough, I figured, and Jail Bait was a sweet girl, I could tell. She was very sweet. I kicked him hard in the balls. I kicked him in the nuts and he fell and I gave him two swift kicks in the face and walked away, listening to him cough and wail and gasp for breath.

***

That night I slept and had a strange dream.

***

When I wake up, I'm all sweaty and I look at my watch. It's only four. I get out of bed and walk to the bathroom where my towel hangs from the door. I shower and open the door to the room, then go out and walk down the hall.

A few orderlies play cards at the table. I sneak by them and wander into the day room where the TV is attached to the wall. I turn it on and put the volume on mute. I don't really want to watch TV, but I don't want to be in my room with Bailey, either. And that makes me hate myself a little. Highlights from game four of the World Series flash across the screen. I watch that for a few minutes and then one of the orderlies comes in to scold me.

Don't you know you should be in bed? he asks.

I want to say, *I would if I were four instead of thirty, you pencil-dicked fuck*! but instead say, *Couldn't sleep.*

What are you watching? he asks, sitting down.

Nothing. Just flipping around.

I heard about your dad, man, fucking sucks, he says, like he knew the guy.

Yeah. What're you gonna do?

You feel like talking about it?

I do! I do I do I do! Please, ask me again because I need to tell someone how much I'm hurt and scared and bitter and angry and how much I miss the only person in my life who truly meant anything to me! I really, honestly need to tell someone and by God, you'll do just fine! But instead, I say, *Naw. Not really. You're right, though. It does suck.*

I laugh so I won't cry right here and now. Then I cry hard and loud and a lot of people wake up and come to their doors to see what's going on. And I'm howling like a fucking dog and laughing and wailing! And it's so funny! It is so fucking funny that I start laughing and laughing until my sides hurt and everything gets dull and misty. Then I start weeping again. Then laugh. Cry, laugh, cry, laugh, etc.

Yes! Yes! Yes!

That's one of my last real memories: laughing and weeping and laughing in the day room at St. Michael's with everyone staring at me, wondering what the hell is so heartbreakingly funny.

Only I knew, and they never would. Neither will you, unless you already do.

***

There's this movie that says if you say you are crazy, then you are not, and visa versa. I thought the book was better.

***

My mom comes at ten this morning and everyone steers clear of me.

Honey, why didn't you comb you hair? she asks me when she walks into my room. Bailey's nowhere in sight. I'm thankful. And I hate myself for it.

I've been really busy.

Come here, she says.

I walk over to her. She spits in her palm and smoothes my hair over. She straightens out my scrubs and kisses me.

How you doing, Mom? I ask.

Well …

She tears up and can't finish. (Sea of regret)

I hug her and we stay in one spot for a few moments, just hugging. Me and Mom, together.

I want you to come home for a while, sugar, she says.

I will.

I don't like it here, she says.

Neither do I.

She sighs and we walk down the hall, she with her handbag and me with my clothes. I'm still wearing the scrubs that they made me wear for three weeks.

Now, the nurse starts, my new doctor standing behind her, hiding behind the words he's given her. *Mr. Dolby will be back in three days, yes?*

Mother looks at me.

And he will stay until the doctor sees fit?

I don't know. We were going to have him transferred to UConn Medical when the grieving is over. That's what we had talked about.

She looks at my new doctor.

We had them on the phone, the nurse is saying. The new doctor nods, begging her to go on. *They won't take him. Your insurance isn't going to cover the initial stay. They want the money up front. You'll be reimbursed.*

Up front? I squeal. *We aren't buying a fucking car—*

Honey, please, my mother says in a shushing tone. *What do you mean by* 'up front'?

Now my new doctor speaks up in his gentleman's voice and says, *My dear, Mr. Dolby suffers from schizo-affective disorder. It's a combination of many serious ailments and he needs hospital care!* He goes on, *However, he has no insurance. Your insurance will cover him, but not right away, there is a process that must be followed, and when it's finalized you'll be reimbursed the expense of his stay. UConn would need the money up front. But you would be reimbursed.*

I could have sworn I asked to leave this shit hole before my own insurance ran out, I hiss, completely baffled and pissed and freaking the fuck out.

The inmates are running the goddamn asylum, **M**om almost mumbles. *I'm taking my son home with me today and we aren't coming back! And that's all there is to it!*

She says this in about four seconds. It's kind of barfed out. Mom is so pissed. So am I. Frustrated. Angry. Fed up.

The doctor looks at me all redfaced and indignant. I lose interest right after he starts talking about staff care or something and then it happens. Now, I have always liked Bailey. I have. He's a swell guy who's walked through shit all his life. I'm looking at my mother. She's looking away. Her face just goes blank with disgustfrightconfusion. Then she starts to tear up, then cry, then weep.

I look to where her wet eyes are set.

And it happens. Bailey is taking a monster dump on some newspapers that are lying on the floor.

Bailey! the nurse yells.

My new doctor rubs his temples.

I thought we had these accidents under control in this ward, he says. *And it was my understanding this patient was going to be questioned and transferred.*

Bailey. Oh, God, no. I want to mourn for him. No one deserves to have a life like this. It's around this time that I decide to stop talking to God. *Bailey,* I whisper. *Why?*

This happens all the time? Mother is almost sobbing. *What did my son do to deserve being sent to this place? What? What kind of place is this?*

Why does life have to be so fucking awful for him? Who the fuck deserves a life like this while jerk-off jock pricks like Beefy Guy get laid in bathrooms?

*Oh, my God, no …*I think to myself.

***

Well, long story short, my mother signed my release and we were out of there for good. My stay at the hospital had ended as it had begun, with a lunatic taking a shit on the floor. And that was about it for me. From that point on, my lucidity and my mind began its downward spiral. No more.

Sometimes memories keep you sane, says Donald. One hell of a memory. My widowed mother. Crying. Weeping. As she watches my roommate Bailey take a shit on the floor. Done.

TWELVE: *I'll Find Them*

In August, I get my driver's license. I had started to learn to drive when I was fourteen—lost my privileges—and so Dad's reteaching me. So I'm with him for most of the summer, relearning how to drive. Best three months of my life. I never see him now that he's remarried. (His wife will die when I'm twenty-two.) People tell me that I'm a loser because I'm still learning to drive at seventeen, and it's almost my eighteenth birthday. But I don't give a shit, I tell them.

At least I'm getting a license, I tell them. *Finally,* I say.

No. Wait—

Is this one?

Yes no yes no—

Wait.

My dad's wife Audrey is a hair dresser, and she and Dad bought me a Nissan Sentra—used—with red paint and black interior. Audrey says it's sleek and sexy, and that I look great driving it. She says this all summer until I actually get my license and then the whole plan turns to shit when on the day I start driving alone, I run into a cop car. A big, burly policeman walks up to me (he was at a diner across the way) and curses me out and writes me a $700 ticket, which takes all the money I've saved all summer. Audrey stops saying how great I am after that.

Since I had my freakout with the marijuana, my friends who aren't my friends won't call me or see me. They won't talk to me, and this is my senior year, so what now? Will I spend the rest of the year by myself?

You fucked up, says Mike one day, two weeks before school starts. *What you did …* He doesn't finish.

I want to remind him that he *wanted* me to smoke up, that he insisted, and I didn't even want to do it. But I don't say anything. I just stand there in the entryway of his house like a fucking idiot. And then he tells me that it would be better if I found new friends. That he and Pat and Keith didn't need cigarettes so badly that they needed me dragging them down—like they're a baseball team and I'm in a slump, fumbling the ball, missing every shot. Like I'm a huge fuckup.

I call Pat. He says he's busy and I ask if he can call me back. He doesn't.

I call Keith and he says that he's working and he'll call me when he's finished, and no, he's not mad, and yes, he wants to do something.

Maybe you and I could go mini-golfing or something, I say to him. *You know, before school starts next week.*

Yeah, he says. *That'd be great,* he says. He tells me he'll call, but he doesn't. No one calls.

I decide to call Mary Ann and she tells me that she's been really busy. And I ask her if she'll go with me to the movies. She says she has to think about it, that she's been so busy lately, but she'll think about it and get back to me. And she does, and says she'd love to go to a movie, that she needs a break.

I need a break anyway, she says.

I'll pick you up, I tell her. *I'm a legal driver now,* I say. I had been known to drive illegally.

We go out. We go out and we go to a lame movie about a man and his pig, and then the two of us get dinner at a small diner in town called the Lookout Diner. It's there that I tell her that I love her. Always have. She says she loves me, too. Always has.

I take her home and we kiss in the car. Long. Tender. Forever.

***

I call Keith to tell him. He says he's in the bathroom, can he call me back? Doesn't. I call Pat to tell him and he says he can't talk, either. Mike says he doesn't give two shits about my love life and hangs up. Mary Ann loves me. But my Mind—Mind with a capital *M*—doesn't see it that way. My Mind tells me that it doesn't matter that I have Mary Ann. For some reason, my goddamn fucking pieceofshit Mind tells me that I need them. I need my friends who aren't my friends and Mary Ann doesn't love me anyway. Never did. Why else would she go so long without talking to me? So it doesn't matter. They hate me, so what's the point?

I walk to the bathroom. I open the medicine cabinet. I take out a bottle of Bayer. I open the bottle. I down the entire contents of the bottle. I wait for death. But it's Bayer, and Bayer doesn't do a goddamn thing, even if you take a whole bottle of the fucking stuff. All I get is a belly ache. So I just sit there on the toilet seat and wait there like an idiot. Then my mom walks in and asks me where the Bayer went and I start to cry. She tells me to put my finger down my throat, and I do, and I throw up all the chewedup pills. Donald takes me to the hospital because Mom is too sad to do it. So we go, and Donald says that he loves me. Says it for the first time ever, and that he's really going to try and be a better brother. I don't know what to say, so I don't say anything. (Sea of regret)

He nods and leaves me at the door of the mental ward of the hospital where the orderly tells me to walk inside. *Go through the doors and walk inside,* he says. *Here's your room. You can set your bags over there,* he says.

My roommate is Steve. I know him. He goes to my school. He asks me what I did to get myself stuck in here. *What did you do*? he wants to know. *Guy like you probably tried to slit his fucking wrists.*

I took a bottle of aspirin, I say, hoping that it's manly enough.

Pills? Like Marilyn Monroe? Figures.

I want to ask him, what the fuck is that supposed to mean? *"Figures?"* I want to ask him who the fuck does he think he is, that we're all in the same boat here. That just because he's scared as hell doesn't mean he has to be a dick about it. But I don't say anything. I just stand there like a fucking fool and wait for him to say something.

Fag , he says softly, then goes to take a piss.

***

By the time I wake up the next morning, the entire floor knows how I tried to die. It's a goddamn dickmeasuring contest with guys when they're in a mental hospital. How you try to kill yourself will determine how you are perceived.

I lit myself on fire …

I drank Drano …

I stabbed myself thirty-seven times, shot myself twice in the head, and all the while I was hanging by the neck from the rafters in my parent's garage.

I took pills, and they think it's too terribly funny for words. *Fag, faggot, butt-fucker, ass-pirate, fudge-packer, turd-tickler, etc., etc.* All this and more. I'm gay. Trying to die by taking pills apparently means you also enjoy anal sex and rim jobs. Who knew? I certainly didn't.

The only person who talks to me is a fifteen year-old girl named Donna who slit her wrists and feels the need to show them to me once or twice an hour. Shows me the stitches and shows me the gash that seems to wrap around her entire wrist. The wounds look like plants—cacti or something—and every time I look at them, I get nauseated. She doesn't pick up on this.

We play cards in the day room while the guys talk about what a faggot I am, what a dildo, what a douche, what a loser I am. I can't figure out for the life of me why no one likes me. Is it my hair cut? Is it my clothes? Is it my face? Is it my voice? Is it my family? Is it my car? Is it my politics? Is it my hobbies? Is it my taste in music, TV, films? And would someone please tell me what the fuck is so wrong with me that no one wants to even talk to me, to get to know me at all? Because I'll change, God damn it!

What the fuck did I do to you anyway? I want to know. *Who are you to judge me?* I ask the world. *What about* my *eraser?* I demand.

On the anniversary of my sister's death, Mom comes to visit. She tells me that Donald is not doing well. That Donald blames himself for what happened. That he feels responsible. That he feels like he should have taken better care of me. Been a better big brother. Looked out. Seen the signs. And I want her to ask him why he feels responsible. That he has enough to worry about. That his life is complicated enough without worrying about his little brother. That there is nothing he can do, really, and no matter what, I'll still feel this way. That there is absolutely no cure for this. That I'll always be weird inside. That I'll always have this. That there is no antidote for crazy.

But I don't. And I hate myself for it. (Sea of regret)

I don't want Mom to leave, but she does anyway, because visiting time is over. So I sit back in my bed and read a biography of John Lennon and eat Little Debbie's until an orderly comes into the room and tells me I have a phone call. I walk to the pay phones and hear Mary Ann asking me how I'm doing. Am I okay? She's so worried. She loves me so much and she's so worried and how could I do this? How selfish am I? What would she have done if I'd actually—

I'm sorry, I say.

Well, you damn well better be! she shouts.

We only talk for five minutes when she has to go. And she goes. And I'm stuck in this hospital again. Donna comes over and starts flirting with me, shows me her wrists, and then I go to bed.

***

I dream about Suzanne. I dream about that day at the river—sun, .25¢. She asked me about the penguins, why I liked them so much. I told her, *Because they can't fly away,* words to that effect. But now I feel differently. Now I can't stand penguins for that very reason. They just sit there. They just sit there, eat fish, and swim. I know they can't fly away because they're too big and clumsy, but they don't even try. I find them cowardly, suddenly. I find them weak and worthless.

And for the past ten years, every goddamn time I see a penguin, I think of my dead sister. And I think of how much I still miss her voice, her smell, her hands. I miss my sister so much that some nights—nights like tonight—I cry and cry and cry until I'm spent, until I'm all dried up, until Steve tells me to stop crying, calls me a faggot. I don't even hear him. I'm wrapped in Suzanne's arms. I'm safe in her memory.

And I just don't give a shit anymore.

**

Me: *How is Donald?*

Mother: *Your room is a study now. You'll have to sleep in the guest room.*

Me: *Mom. Donald. Is he okay?*

Mother: *Your brother is not dealing with it very well, no.*

Me: *Does he think it's his fault? Because it isn't.*

Mother: *He isn't taking it well.*

Me: *Does he blame himself?*

Mother:

Me: *Mom?*

Mother:

Me: *Mom. He doesn't blame himself for all this shit, does he?*

Mother: *Don't say that word.*

Me: *For fuck's sake! Does he think this is his fault?*

Mother:

***

As we take exit thirty-four on I-95, ten minutes from home, mother decides that it's time, finally, to discuss what's been going on. *First, you almost go to jail, and then you quit your job, and then you get sent to a mental hospital. What's next? A cult, maybe?*

Hesitating: *Things are getting weird.* I debate whether or not I want to get into this with her. I realize that I do. *I feel … fuzzy. Like I'm not quite all there. My brain won't stop screaming.*

My hands feel around in my pockets as I tell Mom what's been going on. Terror. Frustration. Confusion. Worry.

Well, you're through with hospitals for a while, okay?

I feel the pages of the prescriptions.

***

We pull into the driveway and I see Donald walking crisply towards the car. He waves and smiles and comes to the window, puts his arms on the glass, says hello.

Hello, he says. *How're you feeling?*

I nod. That's my answer.

How are you? I ask him.

He glances at the ground, then the sky. *Fair. Not great. Miss him already.*

I nod. That's my reply.

You want to get some coffee later? I look at his face, into his eyes, and see a plea. He smiles at me and I just stare at him, and I hate myself for it. *It might be nice.*

Yeah. I'm going to take a nap first.

I'll wait. You sure you're okay now? I was really worried. It's not fair, this stuff always happening to you, you know?

I want to tell him that I'm not okay. That I feel like shit. That my life is crumbling all around me. That I want him to make it better. That I want him to hug me, hug me like Dad used to. Just tell me it's all going to be okay. Like before. Like way, way before, when we were a real family. I need to hear it. Tell me that! Tell me tell me tell me! But I say nothing. I don't say a fucking word. (Sea of regret)

Mom asks me for the prescriptions. I hand them over to her and we both get out of the car. Donald gets my bags and I go inside the house. Dexter is not there. I imagine he's not working somewhere outside. Like in the hammock or something. Even now, in November, I'm sure he's in his fucking hammock like the deadbeat he is. He's a retired cop, so I guess he thinks that since he used to be the long arm of justice he gets to sit on his ass all day and drink rum and Cokes while reading mindless thrillers that all have the same plot while my mother tries to keep their heads above water with her social security and a job at the local beauty salon—fuck you, Dexter Manning!

I head up to the guest room, sit down on the pullout bed, and stare at the bookshelves lining the wall. Standing, I go over to the first shelf and see my old junior high year book. Glenview Park Junior High. The book is somewhat battered by the almost fifteen years that have passed since junior high wherein the book was probably in the basement underneath the radiator, because that's a great place for it—fifty dollars well spent. Page one is of the ninth grade class. I know what's coming. And I don't care. I flip to the M's and find her. With her braces, acne, bad hair. I see Mary Ann. She's so sweet looking, almost helpless. She watches me from the page. I don't want to look, but I have to. Must. No choice. She seems to claw at the back of my eyes, begging me to shut them. Don't look at me. Not now! No—

Donald walks in to find me crying in a heap on the floor. He crouches down and puts a hand on my back. *What's going on, buddy?*

I hand him the book and he says nothing. I'm crying, my eyes blurred, and I assume he knows. But he may not. And I don't care. I'm just glad he's here with me.

I need coffee, I say between gasps for breath.

Sure. Let's go.

Let's get coffee. Please.

He bends down and puts a hand on my head. *Yeah, buddy. Let's go. What're you looking at?*

***

Andrew P. H. Clyde

I tell him what I remember about her. About the baby in her belly, the ring on her finger, the way we kept it secret. Didn't want anyone to know about the baby. Didn't want added stress, wanted a future, wanted the Good Life.

Why didn't you tell me? he wants to know.

I couldn't. I just couldn't.

You should have told someone. Do her parents know? I mean … Donald glances around the diner, rubs the rim of his mug with his thumb. *They really ought to know. It's going to be painful, but you were going to marry their daughter, and you were having a frigging child together. The least you could do is tell them. With all due respect, it's your responsibility.*

I stare at him. *Will you come with me?*

He slowly shakes his head. *I can't. You know I can't. This is your journey. You have to get through this. Losing Dad was hard enough. But two people in a month? Geez, that's unfair. You're a brave guy, you know that?*

I say nothing.

Wait till after the funeral, though. Then you can take my car. I'll be here with Mom for a while with Leigh and the kids until the holidays, so just bring it back in one piece, okay?

We look deep into each other and I see all the years of anger he felt about himself. All the ways he fucked up with me as a brother. And I want to tell him that *nothing* about what my life was or has become is his fault. I want him to know that he was the best brother anyone could have. That he always looked out for me and it was *me* who fucked everything up. And as I look at him, at that moment, I love him so much. I see that he still wants to protect me, and I feel like being protected.

Okay. Okay. I smile at him. *Right. One piece.*

Where do they live, do you know? he asks me.

No. But I'll find them.

You're going to go?

I nod. That's my answer.

THIRTEEN: *When Is It Going to Be Enough, You Sorry Son of a Bitch?*

The funeral is really fucking sad.

Hurt. Anger. Heartache. (Sea of regret)

***

Your meds are at the pharmacy, Mom informs me the day I'm to leave. I've been keeping sane by using the samples from the hospital. *Take my Mastercard.*

I take the card. *Can you get them? I have to go to the bank.*

Or you could pick them up yourself.

I'll pick them up on my way out.

What medication have you been taking?

Free samples.

Well, have you taken them today?

Uh … I've forgotten. The last two days I've forgotten.
I will later.

She smiles and touches my face. *Brave boy,* she
whispers.

I don't know what to say. And that makes me hate
myself.

***

I have $1,300 in a savings account I haven't touched
in over ten years. So, going to the bank to get it was
something of a rush, like opening a birthday card that
has accrued interest by 288 percent. I get the money and
get my medication at the CVS. Back in the car, I have a
small pharmacy in itself lying in a heap on the passenger
seat. Bag after bag of anti-psychotics and anti-depressants:
a cocktail of sanity.

Fill the pillbox. Pack the car. Say goodbye. Get in
the car.

I feel weird.

Mom and Dexter are at the door waving goodbye. It
was Mother who got me the number of Marianne's mom
and dad. They live in New Mexico, near Albuquerque. Or
thereabouts. They didn't know who I was when I called,
and when I told them that I was Marianne's boyfriend,
they didn't know what I was talking about. They actually
hung up on me. Just as well. Secrets are secrets. Marianne
was better at keeping them than I am. Always was.

The car starts and Donald comes between Mom and Dexter. He's holding Maxine, my niece. She waves goodbye to her crazy uncle. And then Leigh walks out the door with a plate of cookies or brownies or somesuch, and runs over to Donald's car. She gives me a kiss on the forehead and hands me what turns out to be pumpkin bars.

Be careful, she says.

I nod.

She walks back to her family. I drive away from mine.

***

I'm almost at the state border and I feel off. I just feel somewhat …off. Can't explain it other than my mind feels like cotton candy and my mood is going from despondent to angry. I have forgotten the cell phone my mother wanted me to have. It's on the kitchen counter. I have forgotten my iPod. It's on the pull-out bed in the guest room. But, and I checked when I stopped for gas in Danbury, I have my meds. They're in one of those cases, the ones with the first letter of the day of the week on each day's dosage. As I cross into New York state, I figure that I should take my nighttime dosage of pills now, even though it's only three in the afternoon, because I haven't taken my pills in two days.

Picking up the case thingy, I open the lid of Monday (with a capital M) and just as I take the whole thing and try to slide them all into my mouth, some fucker in front of me decides that the accident in 84 eastbound is far more important than the road in front of him, and he slows almost to a dead stop. I glance up and slam on the brakes. Screeching tires. Horns behind me. I curse loudly and the other car drives off.

As Donald's car lurches to a stop and the sounds of hundreds of motorists echo in my ears, the medicine case flips out of my hand and hits the dashboard, all of the pills therein plopping and spattering to the floor of Donald's car, dancing like popcorn at my feet, going under the seat and under the pedals and into the radio console, thus making me curse and swear and cuss louder than before. I reach down to pick some random pills from the floor, but the cars behind me are going ape-shit.

Fuck you all up the ass! I'm livid. I curse and hit the wheel over and over with my palms. *Shit! Shitshitshit! Fuck!*

Ten miles later, Donald's car starts sputtering and stalling—more horns, more angry drivers (fuck them all)—and so I get off at Middletown and head to a Midas station to have them look at the car. Before getting out of the car, I look for one pill from each prescription. One lamotrigine, one lithium, one Abilify, on and on.

I come up with lamotrigine and one Abilify and none of the others.

Two are better than not two, so I take them and give the nice gentleman my car. Two and a half hours later, the car is returned, sparkling clean and smelling like peaches and Armor-All. Sparkling clean. As in vacuumed. God damn it to fucking hell, all my pills have been sucked into oblivion!

All sorts of funky shit in this car. Little pieces of candy. Looked like SweetTarts and Certs to me. Got the thing nice and fresh and clean for you. Good as new. The carburetor was fucked pretty much, but it wasn't bad. It's going to be about three hundred dollars.

I glare at him.

Did the funky shit you sucked up look like medication, by chance?

Yeah, I guess it did.

I glare at him. My whole body is screaming.

Did it occur to you to ask me about them before sucking up $1,500 worth of meds in your goddamn industrial-strength vacuum cleaner?

No, not really. Will that be cash, check or credit?

***

Now they have a reason to hate me. They hate me because people like me now. Now that I'm out of the mental hospital people treat me better, with kid gloves. And now Mike and Pat and Keith hate me. But still let me hang out with them because I do things like steal cigarettes and give them beer. And people like me. It's cool to be my friend now. I don't like Mike and Pat and Keith, but still let them hang out with me because they go to cool places like dances and parties and football games and social functions of that nature.

I get to school, though, and they hate me again, and I hate them again, and we all hate each other, but stay together for our own selfish purposes. But in the end, we just don't care if the other drops dead.

***

Students can go off campus for lunch, anywhere in Glenview Park, anywhere at all: uptown to the market, downtown to the diner, across town to the other diner, next door to the McDonalds. I'm not allowed to go off campus for lunch—too dangerous, Mom says. I usually go anyway. I usually take my money and go to the McDonalds.

Yes, McDonalds!

This is—

Yes yes yes yes!

I eat until I get sick with Big Mac. And Mother is none the wiser. My lunch is during fifth hour, hers—Mary Ann's—is during fourth; therefore, I can't have lunch with her, so I don't. Instead I meet up with Mike and Pat and Keith and we walk to the McDonalds and order shitinawrapper, and sit down to eat. I eat in complete silence because who wants to hear me talk anyway? Who wants to hear some idiot, weepy freakyfreak whine about his sister, or whine about school, or his family, or the fact that he's sad all the time? *Why won't someone just listen to me?*

So Mike and Pat and Keith are sitting there, talking about tits and asses and who has the best thereof, until I say to them, I say, *What the fuck?*

And they stare at me, like I just asked them to rub salve on my nipples.

What? asks Mike. He hates me, I can tell.

I said, what. The. Fuck?

What the fuck are you talking about? asks Pat.

Exactly, I say and take a bite out of my Big Mac that would choke a donkey.

My God, you're a freak. This is Keith.

Whatever, says Mike, and they start talking about Daphne Moyer's fine ass, and Debbie Schneider's amazing rack of tits. Somesuch and whatall.

But I don't understand and say it again, *What the fuck!* The three stare at me. I stare back. They want to know what the fuck? And again I say, *Exactly!* And they want to know what I mean, and I say, I say, *What I mean is why the fuck are we talking about this? You know ...* I shove my tray aside. *I just read a book called* Crime and Punishment *by Dostoyevsky for English, and it was good. It was really good, and instead of talking about a good book I read, I'm listening to you three talk about tits and ass, and it's getting old, because that's all you three talk about.* (Where did you find your testicles?)

They are indignant now, and they all shake their heads.

When did you grow your balls, Dolby? The nut house? asks Mike finally, not even picking up on his pun. Fucking idiot. He decides to repeat himself for some reason: *Nut house?*

Fucking nut house, Keith mutters.

Mike takes a bite of his somethingnugget and smiles. *We liked you more when you were a pussy.*

Fucking pussy, Keith mutters.

You think you can talk to us like you're some kind of ... of ... (Think, Mike, think think think) *...of fucking ...like you're better than us?*

Seriously, Keith mutters.

Well, let me tell you something, Dolby, you're a fucking freak! Everyone knows it, and the only reason people are even talking to you is because of us. Because of Pat and me and Keith. So fuck you and your fucking Dusty Esty.

Right, Keith mutters.

Mary Ann likes me, I say. Then repeat it, twice.

I hate Mike, I can tell.

Bite off, Dolby, Pat says at last. He's been keeping quiet and subdued, grasping for phrases and putdowns to put me in my place. Fucker.

And so I bite off. I stand up and walk away, knowing suddenly that Mike was right, and realizing that I'll be alone again for the foreseeable future. Alone. And I know it now, I know that I'll be alone forever. But maybe not. Maybe not. There's always Mary Ann.

I think of Mary Ann.

***

Whatnow whatnow whatnow?

Yes!

Wait—

Yes!

Okayokayokay—

I'm walking to study hall and who should be walking towards me but Mike, bastard Mike who doesn't like me (I can tell), and he's talking to a girl, Daphne Moyer; her newborn breasts are bouncing and jiggling in her loose shirt. It's like she grew them between lunch and fifth hour. Mike keeps glancing at them as he walks along, maybe hoping that they will free themselves of Daphne's chest and spring forth, into his face or hands or dick. Whichever. While she acts like she doesn't notice his boob-gazing, I know she does. She puffs out her chest like a fucking balloon or paper bag. So they walk, and I'm walking towards them. Daphne sees me and smiles. I blush. She looks like an angel, Daphne does, and for a second, I have dirty thoughts of her on me and me in her, but they pass quickly, and once again, I'm clothed and decent. She's coming, four feet from me.

Hey, she says, smiling smiling smiling.

I nod. *Hi.* Blushing blood red. Rising in pants.

She stops walking while Mike is staring at her boobs, saying, *I'm not like other guys, Daphne. I'm really not. I care about you. Jesus, what makes you think that all I wanna do is feel you up? Christ! Well, I guess—*

Hi, how are you? she says to me.

Mike stops talking suddenly, looks up, glares, and says, *Oh, Dolby, when you going back to the funny farm?*

Daphne glances at Mike like steel and her left eye twitches, that's how much she hates him. Good. *Don't listen to him,* she says to me, real soft—like a quilt.

I don't. I smile at Mike. *I never listen him.*

Now Mike's pissed off and he looks down at me, and says to me, he says he says he says, *Why don't you go infect someone else? Leave us be.*

Yes!

This is a good one—

Yes no yes yes—

What are you doing after school? Daphne asks me.

Mike's eyes are nearly bouncing on the floor as I tell her, *Nothing.*

Good, you wanna come over for a while? To my house, I mean.

I think of Mary Ann and don't care, because Daphne wants me to come over, and I know what that means. Boobfest! And only I'm invited, and so only I'll be feeling Daphne's melonbreasts. And so after school I wander the halls to Daphne's locker and who should be there but Mike, who glares and glares but doesn't hurt me because I don't care if he's mad, and also I'm the one who's going home with Daphne, not him, so he can glare all the fuck he wants! Daphne's looking at me, smiling, taking my hand, walking with me down the hallway and out the door, and I don't even look to see Mike watching us. Which he is. I know I know I know he is! And I love it!

Down the street and over two blocks to Maple Drive, through a backyard and onto Spruce, over to Hazel, across the street and through another yard until we get to Daphne's house, a small monstrosity with two stories, and a onecar garage, as opposed to my mother's threecar garage. There is a dog tied up to a long chain—a little mutt with long, flipfloppy ears and something like gold fur. Daphne has been holding my hand the entire walk over and she's been telling me things, like that I'm different than the other guys I hang out with, Mike and Pat and Keith, and she likes me, do I like her, she wants to know.

I do, I say. I promise! Yes I do and I want to touch them now!

She wants to know if I've ever kissed a girl.

I decide to lie. *No.*

She says to come inside. That she'll show me how. And she does. We walk through the front doors and see that no one's home, just us, and she takes my face in her hands and pulls—drags—me into her, not kicking and screaming, but almost.

I think about Mary Ann and how badly this will kill her. She has boobs. And I touch them. But she doesn't have boobs like this. She had nubbinbreasts, not melonbreasts.

I'm scared and afraid that she's going to see my boner. And she does. She smiles and kisses me again, and then puts my hand on her boob. It feels squishy, like a balloon filled with sand.

She puts my hand on her boob and says, she says, *Do you like that?*

What else can I tell her, but, *Uuuuuggghhh.*

And that's when it happens. I feel it suddenly—the uncontrollable tingle that starts in my thighs and works its way to my crotch, where the warmth takes over, I feel I feel I feel the ooze squirming up my privates, and she doesn't say anything because she doesn't know what's going on. She has her eyes closed, and she has my face in one hand and the other hand holding mine on her breast. The warmandtingly builds and builds and I pull into her and feel myself rubbing against her and I start to groan, *Uuuuuuggggggghhhhh,* and feel the warmthencool goo on my leg.

Now she notices.

Jesus Christ! she screams, throwing me back.

I'm so embarrassed that I almost wish I was dead. Almost. And if I was to die, good! Fucking great! Let this be the last thing that ever happened to me.

I go to the door. *I'll go.*

Good! she hollers. *Get the hell out of here, creep!*

I leave, feeling smoosh dribbling down my leg. Totally worth the embarrassment.

***

By the next day, everyone knows about my little pants debacle, and that I came in my pants just by holding Daphne's breast, and what a fucking loser, that he'd come just by touching a breast, and he must not have much experience with women, right? Or you're a faggot (if that makes any sense). That's the only explanation, you fucking faggot freak.

When Mary Ann finds out she won't talk to me, won't even look at me anymore. I have no one now. Alone. Again. Naturally. Goddamn Daphne's enormous breasts.

***

By the time I reach the Pennsylvania border, I feel utterly hapless and discombobulated. Completely spastic and volatile. I start shaking, my mouth twitching.

Able to do it, prove it! (What?)

No no no, nothing like that. Nothing likethatatall.
(What? Whatwhatwhat?)

What? When? Did I do that? No, he's dead. You should know me by—

Able to do it, prove it.

My mind starts doing summersaults and incoherent flipflops and dives and soon I can't see see see straight, so I stop in Scranton and get to a Wendy's. A square booger is in order. So I go to the drivethrough and I wait for a good three minutes.

We'll be—with you—

We—right—you—

W—ri—wi—you—

Garbled mishmush they pass off as English. I'm getting fucking antsy and I need air, I need air right fucking now! Opening the windows, I take a breath of that heavenly Scranton air, and feel sick to my stomach.

Welcome to—how can—you?

I'd like a classic double. Root beer. Fries.

I'm sorry—double—fries?

Classic double, root beer, fries.

Cla—beer and a—would you like to biggie—that?

No!

Please—the sec—dow.

I cringe and drive around to the sececond window and wait for the nice young lady to come for my money—the money that's almost a fourth gone because this fucking car decided to play dead on me. Fucking A!

That's going to be five nineteen.

I give her the money. *Oh, you actually do speak English!*

Excuse me?

Nothing.

I'll get the manager, she tells me, and moments later, comes back with another teenager, this one looking to be about fourteen. Living large in a managerial position so young in life. Good for him. Cocksucker.

Sir, is there a problem?

No problem. I was making an observation. That's all. About the intercom system. Makes your voices all fucked.

Sir, I'm going to ask you to leave.

I want my food.

Sir, I will call the authorities.

Who? The joke police? Give me my food and I'll be on my merry fucking way.

No meds makes me boldcoldold. Stronger. Faster. Smarter. Who needs them? This is a lot of fun, I can do anything!

Denise, call the police.

Fuck you both, I say and drive off, realizing that they neglected to give me my food or change.

There is a McDonalds at the other end of the strip mall, and I go over there. My hands are shaking and I think maybe I need to buy something and that will take the edge off. I feel so goddamned nerved that I almost drive past it.

I park Donald's car and go in, finding a long line reaching almost blackback to the dining area. I get in the backblack of the line. I'm very hot. I'm wearing a heavy jacket and my nose is stuffing up. I can feel the air. It's making me itch. Then, as the line moves forward a few feet, I see something skitterscatter across the floor. A mouse. A fucking mouse is attacking me!

Mouse! I yell, and everyone screams and runs for the walls, as if that'll save them.

Then I see something else from out of the corner of my eye, running across the far end of the room.

Over there! There's one over there! I see them. They're coming for me! *They're all over the fucking place!* I scream.

The manager strides over to me with a scowl on his face. *Just what the hell do you think you're doing?*

What do you mean? I run my fingers through my hair and chew my lips. *I'm saving you from a fucking lawsuit, buddy. Health Code violations and whatnot!*

There is no mouse, nor has there ever been a mouse in this restaurant!

First off, McDonald's is not a restaurant! And I saw one …

Get out.

Why? (I'm so hungry.)

I said get out. Now!

Never again. Never again. Never ever ever evereverever again will I do anyone a fucking favor! It's all I can do to keep myself from weeping like a child. I leave and get some chicken at a dirty KFC where the drivethrough is much clearer and I order a few legs of chicken. Then go back on the road. My nerves are tight and I can hardly breathe.

I think of Marianne.

FOURTEEN: *And Then the Buzzing Starts …*

At a stoplight on Lackawanna Avenue in downtown Scranton, I reach into my coat pocket and come out with a business card. Keith Mann Chiropractics. 1555 Jefferson Avenue. Good. I'll stop and say hello. Good times had by all. Yes yes.

But first, I go down Spruce Street and find a coffee shop called Northern Lights, and I get a double espresso. I've never been in a place like this before, not even in New York. The people are hipsters and intellectuals, and you know they all read real books and watch real films, but they aren't snobs about it. I talk to a guy named Conor about the new Philip Roth book for a while, and he doesn't seem like the kind of person who will roll his eyes and make fun of you if you don't like the books or films he likes. He's very real. And he makes me feel like I'm real. I'm not used to that. They're all nice here, and I ask where I can find a bookstore. Conor tells me there's a nice place right around the block. I find the little bookshop down Center Street on the second floor. The place is amazing. Really funky and cozy. It's called Anthology, where a nice woman named Andrea says *Hello, can I help you?* I don't say much, just that I'm looking for a book. She asks which one, and I say I want *The Crucible.* She gets me the book, and Andrea is so nice that I just want to thank her for treating me like a human. Lately, that's become a rarity. I buy some more used books and she says, *Come again,* and I say I will, even though after I'm done talking to Keith Mann I will have no intention of ever returning to Scranton. Ever. I leave Anthology, thanking Andrea, and begin again on my mission.

I roll onto Jefferson and fix my speed at around ten miles per hour (angry drivers, whatall), dying to find my friend who isn't my friend so I can tell him off. Tell him how I feel. Tell him what I really, really feel and then I'll drive off and tell Marianne's mom and dad that they lost a grandchild as well as a daughter.

Why can't I recall—

Hold on! Yes—

Wait, what did she—

Shit! When—

Finally, I find a small building with 1555 spelled in wooden numbers across the top of a signpost that says *Keith Mann Chiro*whatever on it. Stop the car. Get out. Walk to the door. Moment of truth. Twelve years of holding it in. Twelve fucking years. *Twelve fucking years!*

Should I be feeling like this?

I go inside. I look around. Posh digs. Keith's assistant is at the desk typing. She looks up when I come in and she smiles and asks me if I have an appointment.

Do you have an appointment? she asks.

No-yes! No! I have to talk to Keith.

Okay, is this an emergency?

Yes. Emergency egermancy. Go get him! Need to talk now!

Whom, may I ask, is he seeing?"

Tell him it's me. That it's—

Just then, an office door opens and Keith Mann walks into the lobby, looks at me, and smiles.

Hey, man! How are you? What the hell are you—

Save the fucking small talk, man. I have something to say—to say to you.

Okay. What's up?

My God, as if you don't know. As if you don't rememember what you did to me—to you to me to me! As if the last twelve years make the previous twelve years fucking stricken from the record! You're a fucking son of a bitch and you ruined my fucking childlife. You and that fucking prick Mike and that nobody Pat, the three of you, picking on me until I cried, making me feel small, making me hurt inside until I bled tears—you fucking—fucking prick! And you sit there and ask me what's up? I'll tell you what's up—I'm in fucking hell right now because I was enraged-engaged to Marianne, you know—the only friend I ever had?—and she's fucking dead and gone and now all I have left are memories. Memories! Sometimes memories keep you sane, says Donald. Memories of you and Mike and Pat and Suzanne and Mom and Dad and Dexter and Donald and you you you, Keith Mann! Memories of you tormenting me and she's dead and she's gone!

I'm crying. The receptionist is aghast. Keith has a strange, angryconfusedfrightened look on his face. At first, it looks like he's going to say something nice, words to comfort and heal. But no. He isn't like that and he never was.

Now, you listen, you fucking freaky fuck, he says, walking towards me. *You come into my office, and you ream me out? Fuck no! I'll tell you something. The reason no one likes you is because you're a fucking drag, man. You make everyone feel shitty. You're a fucking downer! You want to know the truth? I have no fucking clue who this Marianne is. I was being nice. I asked you to coffee because it was a nice gesture. Now get the hell out of my office before I call the police, you sorry shitfaced fuck ...*

***

I drive down I-80 with tears running down my face and snot streaming from my nose.

Why? Why? Why? Why? Why? Why? Why? Why? Why? Why? Why? Why why why why whywhywhywhy ...?

Why me?

Why does all the shit have to happen to me? How long do I have to put up with this? When is it going to be enough, you sorry son of a bitch?

***

I'm nearing State College, Pennsylvania, and my mind is reeling, but calming. I feel so awful that I'm having trouble being alive. I hate the world for what's it's done to me, and what it's doing to people like me. I hate indifference. I hate ignorance. I hate the lack of empathy. I hate the lack of decency. Decency that comes with cancer and AIDS and Parkinson's and MS and TB and diabetes. But is absent from mental illness. I'm sick and tired. I'm fed up and frustrated.

I need to sleep.

***

At first, I'm fine.

Fuck it, I think to myself cheerily, as if I wasn't completely psychotic. *I never needed them anyway,* I think to myself. Meds are for losers. Crazy people. Nutty buddies. Of course, by the time I'm in Youngstown, Ohio, I'm pulling my fucking hair out by the roots and yammering about my dead father.

And then the buzzing starts.

Buzzing, the silence has a buzzing quality—not like a bee, necessarily—but not quite unlike a refrigerator.

As I drive down I-80, I hear three things: the motor, the passing cars, that goddamn buzzing.

Then there's this:

It starts in my gut. I feel empty and at the same time sickeningly full. Like I've had too much coffee. I feel it in my chest: this pressure and anger and violent rage. It's not that I don't need medication. I realize it won't do me any goddamn good. No. I'm pretty fucked right here. I close my eyes as I drive down the interstate until I hear the *gridgridgrid* of the perforated asphalt on the shoulder and slide over to the side of the road. The cars pass. The wind blows. The buzzing buzzes. All I can hear—all I can feel—is buzzing. And sadness. The both of them working together to form this unified force of mental incapacity.

Just start the car …

Just put it in drive …

Just drive it off the road …

Just start the car …

I think of Marianne.

I start bashing my head against the steering wheel, shouting, screaming, screaming, screaming …

***

There's a knock on my window and I open my eyes. How long have I been here?

Sir? a big, pile of a state trooper says. *Could you roll down your window?* (I do) *Can I see your license and registration, please?*

Why? I watch the cars pass me from the side of the road. *Was I speeding?*

He leans in. *You can't park here and I don't appreciate the sarcasm. Now, your license and registration.*

I flip through my brother's owner's manual and find everything I need, then hand my license over.

It's my brother's car.

Yeah, he says. *We'll see.*

Grunting, he walks away. After fifteen minutes of waiting, the guy comes by and gives me everything back. *Don't park on the side of the road again,* he says to me, then starts to walk back to his cruiser.

I wait a moment for him to drive away, the buzzing in my head growing to a fever pitch. Getting tired of waiting, I pull out onto the road, only to see him pulling out as well, tailing me for about five miles until I pull over again. He does the same. I stop the car; he does as well, then gets out and almost sprints over to my car.

Son, what in God's name do you think you're doing? Did I not tell you to stay off the goddamn shoulder?

I was nervous with you riding me like that. I probably shouldn't have said that.

Riding you like what?

Like a fucking prison rapist, I want to say …then realize that I actually did say it.

You little sonuva—

He opens my door and pulls me out. Throwing me against the hood, clasping handcuffs on me.

All I asked is for you to stay off the goddamn shoulder and you—fuck! I hate you punks! And he leads me to his car and tosses me inside the back, drives off, leaving the car on the shoulder of the road.

I don't feel the need to point out the irony of the situation.

***

My skin crawls as I sit in the pen. The pile of a state trooper stands over the desk to my right, badmouthing me to his supervisor. The clerk across from him keeps glancing over at me and nodding. Not knowing what the hell is going on is the biggest frustration of all. The officer walks past my cell and shakes his head. Then the clerk leaves his desk and I'm left alone for a good hour, left to think about what I've done. I'm released at five.

You're free to go, says the clerk.

So I was arrested for no good reason?

Looks that way, doesn't it?

***

Taking a taxi back to my brother's car, there doesn't appear to be anything wrong externally with it—no one's fucked around with the paintjob, windows, tires, etc. I pay the cabbie with cash. All four hours after stopping to cry. Never again. Driving driving driving, I reach the outskirts of Cleveland and get on I-71 headed south. I get off at the Ashland exit and decide to stop for the night. Nighttime is always the best time of day for the Crazies. Always always. The buzzing grows louder.

Maybe a little sleep will clean the cobwebs.

***

I'm in a pit. It's dark. Where am I?

***

I walk into the Fu Manchu Hotel and Bar and ask for a room. People stare at me as I drop my overnight bag on the floor. They drink their drinks and eat their pork rinds and chips and pretzels while my mind slowly turns to chickenshit.

My room: to say that the place is a dive is like saying Darth Vader is a little evil. I can smell the cheap sex in the mattress. I know the bed I'm about to lay on is probably still warm and a little moist from the casual fucking that transpired herein moments earlier.

I sleep. Or, rather, try to.

***

I try to sleep.

183

I try to sleep.

I try to sleep.

All work and no play makes Jack a dull boy …

I try to sleep.

I try to sleep.

I try to sleep.

Fuck …

***

At three in the morning, after trying for six hours, I understand that I won't be getting any sleep any time soon. And since I know I won't be sleeping, I might as well be on the road getting closer to Marianne's folks' house. I should start driving again. Getting my things, I leave the room and grab a Snickers bar and a Coke from the vending machines in the entryway.

I get in the car and head south.

***

The pit grows darker and darker and darker and—

***

I feel absolutely numb. I don't feel anything. Nothing. Not high, not low. I feel …pale. The road swoops under me and the lines in the center meld together to form one solid yellow blipblipblip in front of me. It feels like someone is kneading my brain. There's a coin in the center of my head and someone's trying to dig it out.

I can't think of anything.

So I try and focus.

Focus.

Focus …

I think of Marianne.

***

The summer before I go off to college at Albright, Marianne says she needs to tell me something, and would I mind talking. We're at a party. It's graduation night and I'm with Mary Ann. We go off alone into the woods where we can talk in private.

No! Wait—

Yes!

Okay—

It's graduation night. We just spent the evening in the sweaty auditorium of Glenview Park High School—stifling, can't breathe—and then Marianne comes and says she has to tell me something. So that night while we're both drinking, she tells me that she's going to London (or Glasgow) and she's going to go at the end of the summer, going to Suchandsuch University.

I'm not friends with Mike and Pat and Keith anymore. We now officially hate each other. But for some reason, we still find ourselves in the same places, and at some point, we end up either standing around together and pretending I'm not there, or we actually talk. Our friendship that isn't friendship is like herpes. A long, irritating case of herpes. I'm the herpes and I irritate them and pop up at the wrong times and they just wish I'd go away. But I just stick around, some times more noticeable than other times, but I never quite leave. I go off with Mary Ann and they go into remission; but then I miraculously reappear and the itching and burning continues.

Okay, so she's with me and we're drinking and it's graduation night and can we be alone? So we go and she tells me she's going to school in London or Glasgow or Cambridge or Paris or some fucking place, and I'm dying inside. I can see her talking but I'm not listening. It's like she's not even there.

It'd be so great if we could get together, she says.

I say it would be, yes—very, very, very very veryveryvery nice. But I'm dead inside and keep drinking. She sees me crying a little and I ask her why she didn't tell me sooner. She tells me that she doesn't know why she didn't just tell me right away. But she thinks we should stop seeing each other.

No! Please! No, Marianne, I—

We can't do a long distance thing, she says. *It's not fair to either of us.*

But I love you, I've never loved anyone—

I know. I love you, too. But if it's meant to be it'll turn out okay for the both of us. Right?

No!

She says she's sorry. And would I like to kiss her, and I tell her, *No, I have to get home.*

She says she'll drive me. That I've been drinking. So she drives me home and we sit in the driveway of my mother's house and just sit there, the car idling, and I tell her that she shouldn't have done what she did. That it wasn't right.

I'm really sorry, she tells me, real softlike. Like I'm a little child. A baby. And I am, sort of. I feel like as much.

She kisses me and says she should go. I ask her if she loves me. She doesn't answer; she pulls out after I get out of the car, drives off. I won't see her again for some time. Years. And then we fall in love again. And then we go out. And then she dies.

I think—

Yes!

Wait …

FIFTEEN: *Gut-Piercing Cries for Helphelphelp ...*

I drive through Cincinnati and I'm completely convinced I'm going to die. My mind's being held for ransom out here on the open roadoad. The abductors of my sanity laughing and laughing and laughinglaughinglaughing while I rip. My fucking. Hair out. I start hearing my thoughts. They sound like teenytiny screams—tiny screams, gut piercing cries for helphelphelp.

When did this start?

I need to pee ...

I'm hungry ...

Should I stop?

I'm hungry ...

I need to pee ...

When did this start?

Knife …

Hospital …

Shit …

Dad …

Shit …

When did this start?

I guess my last memory is—

I drive and seem to be going in circles. I must be going insane. Loopyloony AndyRooney. It's two in the afternoon and I'm scared. Shitless. In Louisville, I veer off the road and find myself on I-64 driving west and I don't give a shit either way. I'm so fucking pissed off. I'm angry at God Ken Mom Dad Suzanne Donald Marianne Ted Bailey Jesus-Fucking-Christ himself! I don't give a good goddamn! What is this? Why me? Why does it have to be *me* driving out here in Bumblefuck while Keith-Fucking-Mann lives the Good Life in Scranton, Pennsylvania? Why? Why is the good shit left for the bad people, and the bad shit for those who don't deserve it? Why isn't *he* crazy? Why doesn't *he* hear fucking voices? Why didn't *he* try to kill himself? Why didn't he come into *my* office and why didn't I tell *him* off? Life is one misery after another until you just wish everyone was dead! I swear to fucking God, when did life become so unfair? When did—

***

In Dale, Indiana, there's a turnoff and another shitty hotel called Redburt's. I decide to stay and try to get my shit together.

This all means something.

This is all part of the plan.

Get the room. Take my shit upstairs. Lay down. Close my eyes. Fall asleep. Ten minutes later, I'm awake.

***

5:00 p.m.: My head is filled with lead. It keeps tilting and falling forward and backward, and my neck snaps, jump-starting my noggin so that it won't detach from my body. Did I just see another mouse?

***

6:00 p.m.: There's a picture hanging on the wall across from me. It is reflecting my face. I am waving to it and I see this stranger in the picture waving back.

***

7:45 p.m.: Fuck. Fuck. Fuck. Fuck. Fuck. Fuck. Fuck. Fuck. Fuck. Fuck. Fuck. Fuck. Fuck. Fuck. Fuck. Fu—

***

9:00 p.m.: Why the hell can't I sleep? I've been awake for—like—forty hours and I lay down and the bed is comfortable and the sheets and blankets are warm, and yet, I cannot sleep. And what the *fuck* is making me itch?

***

9:38 p.m.: I am no longer depressed. I have moved on to despondent. Maybe melancholy. Simply bored …?

***

10:20 p.m.: I know that I am going to have to check out of this place at noon whether I sleep or not. Am I dead? Am I crazy? No. Not crazy.

***

10:34 p.m.: Fall asleep running the events of the past few months around in my head, trying to make sense of it all. Last thought I have is of a bird flying into a window, trying to get inside a big house.

***

10:54 p.m.: I sleep for twenty minutes. I don't know why I wake up. This is like a dream I had recently. I can't recall it.

***

1:00 a.m.: I stare at the wall and it seems to be moving back and forth, back and forth. I see a little dot that seems to be crawling up and down the wall with each breath I take. What was that dream I had?

***

2:05 a.m.: Fuckfuckfuckfuckfuckfuckfuckfuckfuckf uckfuckfuckfuckfuck—

***

3:09 a.m.: What am I doing?

***

3:10 a.m.: Why did I come out here?

***

3:14 a.m.: Am I going insane? Am I going to die? Both?

***

3:20 a.m.: What am I doing?

***

I finally sleep and have a strange dream. I dream I'm walking over a snake pit, and there's a spider on the floor of the snake pit, and the snakes don't see the spider, but I do, and I shout for the spider to move, to leave, to run off. That the snakes will eat it. Then the spider eats the snakes. Then the snake pit is empty. Then the spider eats me.

I wake up screaming.

It's already eleven in the morning.

***

By 12:30, I'm back on the interstate and everything seems kosher aside from the buzzing that I now hear everywhere. It won't quit, like a friend who just won't get the hint that you really don't want to spend any more time with them.

I turn on the radio and a blues station from St. Louis is playing B.B. King.

He's been downhearted, babe.

Been for a while, in fact. Ever since the day they met.

I think of Marianne.

***

I drink the can of Coke that's in the backseat and it's piss warm and tastes old and tinny. Like drinking a coin collection. I'm far beyond depressed and I feel the mood of the damned coming on—the utterly contemptible feeling of wretched anguish, wrapped up in a neat veneer of feeling sorry for myself. I love that. *Stop feeling sorry for yourself,* as if I can. As if I can turn the selfloathing off like a goddamn light switch.

I don't feel like driving. I don't feel like moving. I can barely breathe. Nothing's going right. What the hell do I tell Marianne's parents? *Hello, how's life without your daughter—oh, by the by, she was carrying my child! Cheers!*

The buzzing drones on and on.

I'm somewhere near the Ozarks when it hits me—I *am*, indeed, losing it out here. I need to buy something. I drive until I see a Wal-Mart sign hanging over the horizon just outside of Springfield, Missouri. Wal-Mart is so awful. It is so God-awful that every time I walk into one I feel the need to destroy it in some way.

I step inside the place—one of those Supercenters with the supermarket and food court and salons and photography shops and restaurants and a ninehole mini-golf course inside, and walk to the music department where I hope to spend some of my savings on DVDs and CDs I will never watch or listen to. But so desperately need.

I pick out some crap from the new releases rack and some shit from the new artists bin and then head to the DVDs, over to drama and comedy and foreign, and there I pick out some classics and old favorites, along with some movies I never really wanted to see, but might as well buy in the offchance I feel like watching them one day.

Going to the electronics department, I pick out an iPod and some blank CDs for when I want to make music mixes. Then I head to the sporting goods department and pick up a baseball glove.

I think of my dad.

Going to the checkout and waiting for an old man to find the $3.50 for the sixpack of Dr. Thunder—waitingwaitingwaiting—I look at the stuff I'm holding and realize that this won't make me feel any better. But then toy with the idea that it might. Who knows?

I get to the register where some skinny guy zaps my clothes. *Beep!* The total is $450. I start to sweat. My underarms and neck and forehead are damp with perspiration. With trembling hands, I reach into my pocket and get my wallet, fork over five hundred dollars, and realize that I have $276 left to get me home. But I can't *not* buy this stuff. I need it on some level and I just can't *not* buy it. So I hand the money over and walk out of the Supercenter with this useless stuff I'll never hear or watch, and I feel worse off than before.

It's now that I remember that I have a credit card. Therefore, by going in and buying stuff on the credit card, I can balance out the cash I spent and all will be well in the state of Wal-Mart. I go back inside and pick up a digital camera, a PlayStation, four more DVDs and seven CDs, for shits 'n giggles, I get a few articles of clothing. Wal-Mart sweaters are fun! I head to Skinny Guy once again, who sees me and smiles as I get to the register.

Do you take credit? I ask and hand him my mom's card.

He's about to run it through when he stops.

Gwen Dolby?

It's my mother's.

I'm sorry, I'm going to have to cut this. This could be stolen.

He says it like a robot. Wal-Mart has made this poor man a cruel, heartless robot! *Look*, I mutter, getting my ID. *Dolby, see? We have the same name.*

I'm sorry, Mr. Dolby. He pulls out the scissors. The checkout. *Beepbeepbeep.*

Give me my card, I tell him. The buzzing gets louder. The anger is building inside. Hate. Utter repulsion. Something bad is about to happen.

Sorry, sir.

I think you need to give me my card. I don't even care anymore. The checkout. *Beep. Beep. Beep. Beepbeepbeep.*

Beepbeepbeepbeepbeepbeep.

He's about to clip my card when I do what I think anyone would do if a Wal-Mart employee was about to cut up his or her credit card. I grab the fascist by the fucking throat and choke him until he drops it! He's on the floor and I grab my card and movies and CDs and camera and whatall and bolt out the door, listening to people scream.

When I get to my car, I hear a man shout, *Hey, asshole!*

I get into Donald's car and back up. There are two people blocking my way. One is a big fat man with a bat, the other is a sullen twenty-something kid with bad skin who looks like he might be so unhappy with where his life has taken him that it really doesn't matter if he stays in the store or confronts me.

Get out of the car! Big Fat Man shouts at me.

I look at the big, fat, tub of goo who now represents everything I hate. He tells me again—*Get the hell out of that car!*—and that's when I accelerate and drive right into him, hitting his left hip with my side mirror. I hear a scream; I think I ran over his foot.

Dumb Skinny Guy was fine and Big Fat Man probably beat his wife. Who the hell cares? I drive recklessly away from the Little Shop of Horrors and get back on I-44, headed west. I'm livid. That just *had* to happen, right? That just *had* to happen, the guy looking at the name on the fucking card—who does that? Some other guy steals someone's credit card and buys $7,000 worth of shit and he gets off unscathed, while I have to strangle someone to—God damn it! God fucking—

Jesus *Christ* that pisses me off. The fucking odds of that happening—my God! I drive off, more angry than I've been the entire trip.

SIXTEEN: *Under a Billboard in Vinita ...*

Dr. Sprat is in her offoffice when I call-all her at eight that evening from a payphone at a diner near Vinita, Oklahoma. It's almost ten in Yew Cork Nity, but she doesn't mind, she says. *I don't mind. I'm glad you called. I haven't heard from you in a while*, she says says says yes yes yes.

For strange reasons I never don't know for certain, I don't want her to know I don't have my medidedication. I think that may be because I don't want her to never tell me to turn around and come home. I also don't want her to think I'm stupidstupid, a stupidish child who's nonot responsibility. So I told her where I am and what I'm doing and who I'll be seeing, and she asks the strangest question. I'm not at all repaired for it.

When did you start seeing Marianne? she wants to know.

I tell her I tell her I tell her I tell her. Junior high school. Duh. Then we took a long break.

But when did you start seeing her again? How did you meet her once you got to New York?

I met her—meeted at this party, okay? A party of a friend of a friend of a friend of a friend and she was there and we started talking and talking and talking and talking and it was like olden times, and I donut know it was her at all at first, but she recogniz-ized me, and asked who I was, and duh, I told her, and so we went out for a drink after the party, and we've been together ever six. Until—

Huh. I see, says Sprat-a-tat-tat.

And she gotted pregnant last summer. And we were going to get married, but no one were supposed to know. I loved her! I fuck-ucking loved her! Now she's dead and you don't believe she veven six-sixted! And then she's dead I I I I don't even know!

I wonder if you could describe Marianne to me. Could you do that?

She had blonde hair. She had blue eyes. She had a big nice smile. She looked like my mother but not in the creepy way. Not in the peepy way deepy way teepy leepy jeepy way—

Huh, she says.

What!

Oh, I don't know. It's just that you never mentioned a Marianne until this past summer, and when you told me about her, you said you'd met at a library. And why didn't you tell me she was pregnant? I would think you'd want to confide something of that magnitude with someone.

I couldn't, I yelltell her. *We wanted to keep it secret. From everyone. She didn't even tell her parents or mother or father or mather.*

Huh, she says.

What! I'm getting so fucking pississed I feel like a bull getting its balls ripped off with a spoon and I just want to gouge some fucking thing.

You didn't even allude to it. Can I ask you something on a different topic?

Yes. I'm seething things.

I want you to tell me if you've been feeling easily agitated. If your thoughts are getting flustered. If you think about something and then your brain starts obsessing and doing flip-flops in the air. Going around in circles.

That bastard motherfucking scissordick doctor mentioned itit tit tit tititit. He mentioned—fuck!

Are you taking your meds? She says it all real serious, like when my mother used to ask if I was drinkinging her beer.

Yes. Yes-yes-yes. I'm taking-waityes! Yes, I'm taking my meds, them-my meds.

Are you?

Yes! Yes-yes-yes!

You're sure?

Fucking yes I'm fucking sure! Fuck!

She's real qu-iet-quiet and she doesn't say anything. I know she knows I'm lying. She always knows. Probably knows what I'm thinking. Take a guess. It rhymes with "trucking bunt!" Sounds just like "dunking punt!" Truck-ucking funt!

I want you to be very careful out there. I want you to call me when you reach Albuquerque. After you see her parents, I want you to call me.

Whatever. She hates me. Always has. From the minute we met. Always hated me. Always always always always always! *Just fucking whatever.*

You sound angry. Are you upset with me?

No intro: *Why doesn't anyone believe me? I just lost the life of my life and people just are treating me like she didn't never exist! Now you don't even believe me that she never fuck-ucking existed! Well fuck you!*

I slamam the phone down. Moments later, I pick it up again and call her moffoffice to tell her off in a fuckload of detail. But the line is business. Minutes pass where I'm seething and fuming and cursing the wind. Then I call homes and my brother picks up. He's frantic and I'm feeling shifty.

Where are you?

Okl-Oklahoma! I think. I think I think I think … I'mI'm here—

202

Stay right where you are! (Save me, Donald) *Go to a hotel and call me back, okay?* (I need my big brother) *I want you to hold tight. I need you to find somewhere to stay and then call me—*

I just talked to Prat, Sprat-Sprattatattat and she doesn't believe—you believe me, right, Donald? You relieve me about My-rianne?

Sure, buddy. I believe you. Are you in a city or a small town? Is there a hotel somewhere?

You relieve me, don't you Donald?

About Marianne?

You believe me, don't you? Right? I'm not lying. Am I?

I believe you. Now go and get a room.

Jack Sprat says she doesn't believe me. I justed talked to her.

I know. She called the house here. I need you to stay inside somewhere until I get there. I'm going to take a plane to Tulsa. Where exactly are you right now?

I see a billboard. Bob's Hunting and Fishing in downtowndown Vinita. I tell him that's where I emminem. Under a billboard in Vinita.

Call me when you get to a hotel!

Okay.

Do it! I mean it! He slows. He calms. *Will you do this for me? Call me when you get to your hotel.*

Okay, but you believe me, don't you?

Go and find a hotel.

He hangs hiccup. I get in the car and continue to drive.

***

My first night at Albright College, I have dream about Suzanne and I wake up screaming. The dream was about that day at the zoo. The spider house. The feely legs. The hand on my shoulder. She's gone. And my dream is that sequence of events played over and over again. The moment I realize that she's gone. Then back to the spider. The hand on my shoulder. She's gone. Over and over again. And I wake up screaming and crying, and my roommate D.J. is sleeping. But not anymore.

What's up? he asks me. *Why you screamin'?*

D.J. is a big football player from Philadelphia.

Bad dream.

'Bout what?

You really want to know?

Sure's hell do. You gonna be screamin' all night all the time, I at least wanna know what you be bawling 'bout.

So I tell him. I tell him about my sister.

***

Suzanne was a bigboned girl, blondehaired girl. She had a tilted smile that was real toothy. She always said she was ugly and that's why I think she liked me. Because I always called her pretty. She was sweet to talk to and she smelled like daffodils. She would take me to the park or the river. She would never treat me bad. She would never treat me like everyone else treated me. Like I was stupid. She never once called me stupid. She never once called me anything bad. She just loved me, and when she killed herself, she killed a part of me as well. And I can't forgive that, but I'll try to. I'll try to forgive her.

When I was in elementary school, the teachers would mutter about my family. My fuckedup family. Some of the kids would tell me that Suzanne was in hell because she killed herself. That only God can take lives. Not people. Fucking Lutherans.

After Suzanne died—about two weeks later—I went into her room for the first time since finding her in the basement. I found a shoebox with pictures inside. Pictures of me and her. Pictures of her and Donald. Pictures of Mom and Dad. But no pictures of friends. She didn't really have any, I guess. Like me.

***

And so I tell D.J. about my sister and he listens and tells me.

That's a fuckin' sad-ass tale, my friend. I wait for him to say something smartass. I wait for him to mock me. To call me some shit that I'm going to have to ignore. Or pretend I don't hear. *Man, that is some fucked-up shit. You seein' someone 'bout this?*

What's that supposed to mean? I'm defensive for no real reason.

I mean, that's some seriously fucked-up shit, an' you should be seein' a psychiatrist or somethin'. Shit, I see one an' my family's the motherfuckin' Huxtables.

I smile.

Come on, man. You need sleep. But I swear, you scream like that again and I be draggin' you to the motherfucking shrink myself. You hear?

I nod.

Good. Now go to sleep.

***

We hang out a lot. D.J. and I are friends and he takes me to parties and to freshman rushes. We drink a little, but he doesn't like to lose control, he says, so he really doesn't drink all that much. Neither do I.

We're friends—good friends—until he leaves and I lose my mind.

It's finals and he's taken his tests and he's getting ready to go home. I still have one more test to take and then I'll go home, too. So I'm studying and he says goodbye and leaves and I watch him walking down the hallway, out the door. I scramble back to the room and watch him get into his Le Baron and drive off. And then my mind starts turning to shit.

I'm drinking coffee and studying and I hear the faintest sound in the back of my head. I assume it's the guys across the hallway. They're a loud bunch of idiots who came to school to meet girls and drink. College is a night club for these people. But they're not there. They already left for Cherry Hill, New Jersey. They went home.

What? You think you can do—

I hear the voice, suddenly, and I become afraid.

You should do it! Yes yes! Do—

I sit up with a start. My mind starts doing summersaults and I start to think funny thoughts.

You're invincible—

You can withstand anything—

Jump out the window—

Do it—

Jump out the window—

You can withstand anything—

You're invincible—

The voice gets louder and louder. I can't hear anything else, not the stereo not the TV not the people in the hallway just the voice and it's telling me to jump and I try not to hear it but it keeps talking to me and I look out the window because maybe the voice is right and D.J. isn't here and I'm alone again and who'd miss me anyway but that's no way to think but it's true and the truth hurts sometimes and there's nothing to do now but wait for the inevitable and you're invincible so just do it do it doitdoitdoit!

And so I do.

***

It's only two stories. I fall into some bushes and break my tibia. Mom and Dad decide to send me back to the hospital. And I go, but no one visits me. I call D.J. but he's not home. No one is ever home at his house. So I'm alone in this strange hospital and I don't know anyone. It's sterile and dark. The people smell of medicine and age. The lights are iridescent. This is supposed to help me?

Finally, I'm let out. Mom decides that I need to stay home and go to school at UConn, Glenview Park campus. So I do.

I don't make any friends. I just go to school and get my work done and work at a small drugstore in town. I never see anyone. I just do my schoolwork and make money at the store. Put the money in a savings account and let it accrue interest.

The next fall, I decide to move. I decide that I'll either move to Los Angeles or New York. I chose New York. It's November. By the new year, my bags are packed and I'm sitting in the front seat of my mother's car, headed for the Big Apple with my shit in a trailer behind us.

***

It's late-ate now and Immime driving in the outerskirts of Oklamoma City. The sky is dark. The moon is out, but I can't see it. I can't see it. I can't see it until I turn my head to the side and watch it watching me from up way there.

The lonely moon.

And in that instant, I am the moon.

SEVENTEEN: *Kafka Kafka Kafka …*

At three in the morning, I stop at fourtofivetosix miles outside of Amarillo at a small diner in a truck-fuck stop just off I-40. My mind is fruitcake parmesan right now, thinking jackass-smackass thoughts, wanting to hurt someonesomethinganything. Feeling invincible. There's melted caramel oozing from my ears and the buzzing is so loud now that I feel literal pain in my head. No thought to me. Just the feeling of not feeling—completely numb. Nothing to be done. Nothing to be done. Nothing to be done.

Yes! Wait, yes! Now I—

Yes yes! This is—

So I walk inside and my Mind must be freaking on Me—with a capital *M*. I see a Wiseman! A fucking Arabic Wiseman sage, robeandall, sitting in the far corner, smoke-toking rising from the table, clouding his face in a hazygauzy sheet. He looks at me and I'm all weak.

This man has the answer! I know I know I know it! This man knows me. I've never met him, but I know him and he knows me like the back of a cloth. He's an outcast. Like me. Never knew friendship. Deep friendship. Lost. Scared. Lonely. Like Me—with a camptimal nem.

I walk to the table and ask to sit down.

He says, *Sure.*

A dark-skinned, Arablooking Wiseman, head wrapped in a towel! A fucking Wiseman! Jesus Christ's Wiseman!

My name is—

Doesn't matter, he says. Motions for me to sit. Something strange going on. *Names are unimportant.*

Do you know me?

What?

Do you know who I am?

Should I?

No, I guess not.

Do you know who you are?

I notice his lips aren't moving. He can see into my soul! He's reading my mind! He just stares at me and I'm hearing his thinks as he spinks them!

I need help, I tell him. He stares at me. *My life is a mess. I'm losing it out here.*

You should find it.

The smoke rises from the table, his face hided behind a veil. He nods and motions for the woman to get him another cup of coffee. He offers me a cigarette and I haven't had one in a while. A long, long while. A longlonglonglong while. It's a peace offering. For his people killing Myrianne. I take the cigarette and he hands me a tighter. He talks without moving his lips—his voice raspy but intelligible.

You know this isn't true. You didn't really know her at all, he says.

What do you mean?

What do you *mean?*

I feel like I've lost the left side of my body.

You have. But not to this Marianne. Marianne is a part of you, but not the part you think, not the part you want, either.

The woman brings coffee for the both of Me. I order plain toast and a glass of water. She nods and walks away, leaving the two of Me alone.

Are you frightened? he asks.

Of what?

Of what is happening to you?

I slowly nod my head. *Petrified,* I say, and I suddenly know it for real.

Once you left your home, you knew you could never go back. Am I correct, white devil?

No. I can go back.

No, you can't. Once you leave, you have left. Like summer after spring, like autumn after summer, and you, friend, are the winter now. The autumn turning to winter. That is what you are. And you cannot go back to spring or summer. You are no longer free.

I'm scared and want to leave. Not right. No no no. Thisisn't at all right.

Why are you staring at me? he asks abruptly, his mouth is moving finally, his voice sounding very much like an Arab. *You have been staring at me for five minutes now. I give you a cigarette and you don't even thank me. You're making me really uncomfortable, even for a white devil.* He lifts the coffee to his lips. *You want something other than toast and water? I'll be happy to get you something. You look lost.*

I am, I tell him. *I am,* I say, and start to cry.

There is an old saying that goes, 'We are all born mad. Some remain so.' *Think about it,* he says. He gets up and lays a ten dollar bill on the table.

Is that an old Arab saying?

He shakes his head. *Samuel Beckett. You be good now,* he says, and wanders out the door as my toast arrives.

***

This is—

Wait—

Yes! Yes! Yes! This is—

I'm driving diving now how. It's six clocks in the morning and I'm already a three ways through New Mexico. There is not much longer how now brown cow. I am almost there. Almost. Almost. *Almost there.*

It's all part of the plan. You should run off the road. You're invincible. It tells me this. The lithiumbuzz in my fucking head. *You should run off the road. It's all part of the plan. You're invincible—*

I stare ahead at the passing desert all a-mound me. I need to pee. I need to pee flee glee. There's an old ass station off the side of the road and I stop and pee and go to the pay phone off to the side of the small building where an old man tits and smokes a cigar, watching me with squinty eyes. Minty pies. Glinty sighs.

I place a collect call to my mother.

Mom mom mom mom mommommom. Nothing doing nothing doing nothing doing …

Hello? Oh my gosh, is that you? Mother has been crying, sighing, and her olive tree is dying.

Mommom-mommy dearest. It's me, Imin the desert.

She's frantic and tantric. *Donald told you to stay in a hotel! He's calling me every ten minutes telling me that no one knows where you are! Now where* are *you?*

I'm right here.

Where are you, baby?

Mom is weeping now—drowning in the tears, drowning drowning drowning.

I'm okay. I'm okay. I'm okay. You know that today is Suzie's anniversary? Mom? You know?

Please, baby, stay there. Donald has some police with him. An ambulance, too. They'll be there in no time. Just tell me where you are.

Suzanne, Mother! Your daughter!

Right, of course, of course. Suzanne, baby. That's right, Suzie … Good, good.

I canner talk in the backcrowd. They're trying to get me! Get me get me getmegetmegetat-tat-tat me! Put me in the hospital again with Wart and Jail Bait and Beefy Guy and shit on the floor and small juice cups and Kafka Kafka Kafka!

I won't do it! I won't go back! (Oh sweet, merciful Christ, make this end.)

A man comes on the line. Dexter Texter Nexter Dexicanexter. Is that who she's talking to?

Hey, kid. Dr. Sprat's on line two. You want to talk to her?

What? Now?—No! No no bono! No I don't! She doesn't-no! Nononono-no-fuckit! Can't do it to it do it knew it!

Wait—

Yes!—

No, wait—

My mind. What? Mind is jump start. Just a little—

Hey, kid. Why don't you just hang tight for a couple of hours until Donald gets there with some help? How's that sound?

You are not my father, Dexter! My dad daddy dad dadadadad …

I know. I'll never take his place. I just—

Hang up! Hang upup the kufucking pony! It starts ringing. The old man s smo-smokoking his cigar and cooking at me. Maybe he knows. Maybe he knows about me. Maybe they all know! Everyone knows and is in on it but me all my life is and has just a joke for them to laugh at me and chuckle and say hahahahahaha look at you you fucking nut damn it you idiot what the fuck such a buzzkill the lithiumbuzz getting louder.

Maybe he'll call someone. Put me in a desert hospital. Maybe. Yes!

Get back inside the car-car carcarcar carcass and turn on the ignortion, peeling out of the sass station before the man can gets to the pony.

***

School in New York City is fun because no one likes me—

No. Wait—

Yes—

Now I—recall—

I don't have a friend in the world but this guy named Jimmy who I don't like much. As I sit in class—writing class—the professor tells me that I lack the quality of a writer. I never wanted to be a writer, I tell him—I did want to be one, but now I don't. Going home on the train to Brooklyn I think hard about the bastard professor and his fucking tweed jacket and black turtleneck and goatee and all he needs is a cigarette holder and a Virginia Slim to make the package complete. Pompous ass. I think about the professor and his tweed faggot jacket and I think of that day with my mother and Dexter. My poor father on the sofa sleeping as the Mets start jumping around because the Sox lost—

Sitting in a seat on the platform at Times Square waiting for the 1/9 train. Waiting and waiting with a book. *The Crucible.* I always read that play. The play is astounding. Astounding with a capital *A*.

So I'm reading and the train comes and I sit on the train and it takes me to Brooklyn and I'm home and I sit down and the phone rings. It's Jimmy and would I like to go to a party with him that Friday? So I say yes and wait for the week to be over because I have yet to go to a New York party. And now I'm going! At the party there's a girl there who looks familiar.

I think of Mary Ann. I go and talk to her. Never the same.

EIGHTEEN: *And so and so and so …*

And so and so and so...

I'm at the party and Marianne is talking and I'm trying to listen, but I'm sinking into her eyes. I'm falling fast into her lovely blues with the gold flecks in the iris. And she talks. She talks and I don't know what I'm supposed to say back—what am I supposed to say when she asks me what I'm up to? Because she knows who I am now, and I know who she is. It went like this:

Where did you go to school? I ask, because I don't want to assume it's Mary Ann. Because then I'd be foolish.

Glenview—Are you—

I don't let her finish. *I am!*

She hugs me.

She kisses my face and says, *It's great to see you,* and, *Sorry for not writing,* and, *Sorry for losing touch,* and, *After all this time, you haven't changed but to look more mature and sexy—*

She says this and I blush and I feel such a pull towards her, such a force that I kiss her suddenly on the mouth, and she kisses me back—

No! Wait—

And—no!—

We're walking through Central Park—no!

We're walking through Union Square, right through the middle of it, and she tells me she loves me. Truly. She says she truly loves me and I tell her that I love her. That I really, really, really do, and that I never want her to be away from me—

***

Jimmy tells me that I'm a lucky man. That if Marianne didn't love me so much, he'd try to steal her away. And he almost tries to one night at another party. The two of them were drunk and they almost kissed, but Marianne stopped and said that she couldn't, and when I heard about it, I was so angry that I couldn't see straight, and that was when I decided to stop talking to Jimmy—which was a shame because he was my only friend.

***

The spring semester is almost over and I'm picking classes for the fall. I've been working at a bookstore for four months, and they fire me because I can't wake up in the morning to get to work. I've never been able to wake up and when they tell me I'm fired, I call my mother and she tells me that that's tough luck, and do I want to move back home? I tell her no.

But this is the fifth job I've had since moving here. I've worked at a tobacco store, I've worked at another bookstore, I've worked as an administrative assistant, I've been a temp, I've been all sorts of things, but never a real employee. And I have no money. And Mom has been paying my rent and I feel like a child. That night, I cry and tell Marianne that I don't want to talk to anyone and I want to die. She tells me not to say fuckedup shit like that. That it would kill her.

I graduate. I get some jobs at agencies and publishers and lose them all one by one. I can't even keep the job I get at the Gap folding jeans and sweaters.

***

Some time later, Marianne tells me that she got a new job. That she's leaving her secretary job at the paper and she's going to work at an ad agency downtown.

In the fucking World Trade Center! she squeals, like that's the pinnacle of success. Working in those fucking towers.

But I'm so excited. I'm so thrilled that I can barely breathe, and I tell her that that's great, and we kiss right there. We kiss right there in the middle of the street, cars passing by, honking their annoyance, pissed off, shut out from our little world. And I don't care at all. I just love this woman and I love this moment, and I just don't care about anything else.

Sickness.

Health.

Poverty.

For better or worse.

***

We're at Manny's—a barrestaurantlounge—and she tells me that she wants to get married to me. One day. Then she tells me why, and I get a sinking feeling in my stomach.

Baby. God. No, I—

***

We decide that for the child's sake, we need to get married right quick. But no one would understand. No one would get it. So we agree to get married in secret. And I tell her that I'll buy her a ring; so I save some money and soon I have enough and I get her a decentsized ring with a nice little stone that she says is all she ever wanted.

It's all I ever wanted! she whispers. And means it.

I worry sometimes. About money and things like that. What with the baby, I say. *I'm scared.* I've never been this frightened of anything. What if the baby is like Me? Me with a capital *M?*

We'll get through this, she says.

Promise?

Promise.

I love you, I tell her.

I love you more than you'll ever know, she says.

***

It's May and I tell her that I need to find a roommate. I tell her—

I need to find a roommate. I can't afford to stay in the apartment otherwise.

She gets upset.

Well, could I move in with you? I ask. *I could break my lease. I could sublet my apartment,* I tell her.

My parents wouldn't have it. They would disown me. Fundamentalists. Evangelicals.

She finally relents and agrees that I should get a roommate.

I interview thirteen people. I choose a guy named Ken Allen because he'll pay more rent than anyone else. He moves in and my life has been shit in a fucking shoe ever since.

***

Memories memories memories. I need them. I have to have to have them. They're there somethere, I know it owe it tow it. They must be, have to be, should be; where the fuck are they?

Sometimes memories keep you sane, says Donald.

Memories of my fucked existence caught in the creases of my brain: Mother holding, Father leaving, boss yelling, everything a memory. Just that. Memory with a capital *M*. So, so, so, what do I recall? What do I know is real? Tell me tell me tell me, because I have to know! You've got to do this, just once! Write them, shout them, think them, but dear God, hurry! Dear God, make it quick because there's not much time now!

No! Please no!

I guess my last real memory is—

I guess—I guess I my last memory was—

Help.

***

I'm here there everywhere. I sit in Donald's car, sitting in the car, sat sit soot in the car on the side of the street, looking at the address. And this is what I see. This is how it will go down:

Wait—

Yes Yes Yes!

No—

Mister and Missus McCormack?

Yes?

I'm—

We know. Thank you for coming. It means a lot to us.

It's really nothing at all. But I can only stay a moment. I can only stay for a minute or two. I have to tell you that there is more to Marianne and myself than you might know.

(Cautious looks. Glances at each other)

What is it?

There was a child.

A what?

A child. She was carrying my baby. Your grandchild. I just thought you had a right to know.

Oh my God! My baby!

My little girl …

My Marianne.

***

Detting out of Gonald's car, I look at the house. All this time. All that's happened and it all comes down to this. It all comes down to this momoment. Intheblinkofaneye. It. All. Comes. To. This.

I step across the lawn.

I ring the doorbell.

I hear footsteps.

The door opens.

And there, standing in front of me with a confused look on her face, is Marianne McCormack.

NINETEEN: *The House of Cheese …*

I stare. I stare. I stare. I stare. I stare. Nothing comes out. No words. What—

Nothing. No words, and just a look from her, older now, much older, by far too many years; bite fart you money ears—much, much older. Fatter face. Thin, limpy-pimpy breasts. Rumpled stilts skin. Nothing like the Marianne I know-knew-no. I ask her something, but no words. No words. No words. Nothing comes out. Like finding Suzie Q. Scream. Just air. No. Words.

She stares at me and squints and almost says something.

Doesn't.

And then the phone in the hallway of her home ringdings and she says, *I have to answer that.* She goes to the phone and picks it up and says, *Hello …yeah, can I call you back?—Great.*

She hangs up and turns to look at me. Learns moo took matt tea. Hang phone learns moo tea. Meturn koottat me. (Oh Jesus, save me)

Then she smiles—

Marcus?

Marianne …

Nothing more comes out. She's dead. This woman is dead. She's dead she's dead she's dead she's dead she's dead she's dead she's dead Goddamn it!

I go by Annie now.

Why? I don't—

Nothing. Why isn't she dead? Why isn't she buried under tons of steel and dirt? Why isn't this woman dead? And who is she if she's not? If she's snot head twat hen? Berry dunder steer heal and hurt. Nothing. Why can't I talk? Wide ant hi taco—

Fuck! You're dead! Marianne, you're fucking dead!

She tilts her head to the side—*Come again?*

Ike ants peak. I'm numb. World is spinning like fuck like spinning the world. Nothing seems to move but this …this …person. Her lips move but I don't hear a fucking word turd bird third.

You're dead.

I'm what?

I stare I stare I stare I stare I stare I stare I stare I stare I stare I stare I stare I stare—what the *fuck* is going on here?

You're dead!

She squints again. This is Marianne. This is Marianne, dammit! This is: *You wanna walk me home? I live on North Main Street. I'm going to school in Glasgow or London or Paris or some fucking place. I love you and I mean it. I love You with a capital—*

Why aren't you dead! I saw you die! You're fucking dead, Marianne!

I don't understand, she says cautiously, as if I—

You're—you died in—I watched it—You called me! Goddamn it, you aren't real! This isn't real!

Marcus, you're beginning to scare me a little.

I start to pace and pace and run my fingers through my hair and pace and pace and run my fingers through my hair and pace and pace and run my fingers through my hair and pace and pace and pace and pace—

No no no no no no no no no—

Over and over I repeat the word, hoping somehow that it will become true. Hoping above all hopes that this woman *is* dead. I need her to be dead! Because if she's alive and I'm seeing her now and she's alive and I'm—

Marcus, please sit down. Are you having an episode? Do you still call them that? Why don't you sit down?

Why are you here— Pace pace pace pace pace …

Why am I here? I haven't seen you in years and that's what you give me? Why am I here? *Jesus, I didn't know you were still this bad. I thought you'd get better after a while—meds and all …*

We don't get *better, Marianne!*

Okay. I'm calling the police.

Tell me where you were on September 11! Tell me that I'm speaking to the ghost of someone who died in the towers—the same towers I saw tumbling to the ground, tumbletumbletumble and crash and dust and smoke and dirt everywhere, memos in the air, emails—

I was in my classroom, Marcus. What the hell is wrong with you?

Put it together. Pull it together put it together push and pull push and push and pull pull pull. That's the way the world works. You get sick, you get better. You break your fucking arm and it heals. Might be weak for a week. But it heals. Break a leg, heals. Get a cold. Gets better. A few Kleenexes later and it's all good. Die! Die, Mary Ann! You die because I don't have a Kleenex big enough for this shit!

Wait!

Not a thing to say at this point. Not a goddamn thing to say.

I heard your voice! I heard you tell me that something had hit your building. I heard the sound of people screaming. I heard you say it—

Well, that it was all in your head, Marcus. Because I haven't been out of Albuquerque in months, and the last time I was out I was at a conference in Tempe. I don't know what you're going for, but if it's to creep me out, success and kudos to you. I'm officially freaked out.

Are you pregnant?

What? That's a fine thing to ask someone—

Are you pregnant! With my child!

Incredulity wipes over her features. I need a Kleenex. Big time. Pig dime. Dig mime.

I want you to leave.

You're dead—you're dead—you're dead, I saw you die, your memory is in my head—

I haven't seen you in years, Marcus! Not once. You stopped talking to me when my dad got the job out here. We haven't spoken to one another until five minutes ago! You and I aren't anything, Marcus. You aren't the father of my child—I don't even know where to begin telling you what's wrong with that statement—and I didn't die in the towers on the eleventh. I was in my classroom with my second graders at Dellwood Elementary. That's where I was. And I've been living with my mom and dad since my divorce a year and a half ago. So I don't know where you get off coming to my home and calling me fat and telling me I should be dead! That's a little creepy, Marcus! This "life" of ours—yours and mine—is all in your head!

I stare and tear and hair and tear hair. No sense. Nonsense. No one knew about Marianne and me because we wanted to keep it a secret. We wanted to keep it under wraps. And my family never listens to me. And I have no friends. We met at a party, or the library or in a classroom or some shit. And this can't all be in my fucking head because that would be impossible! Goddamn it, this is not happening! No no no!

No, you're dead, Marianne! You have to be dead!

Get out!

Get up in her face, spit spattering her. *You have to be dead or else I'm completely fucking nuts! And I'm not completely nuts! I'm not! No matter what they tell you, I'm not a freak! I'm not a freak and I'm not a liar! I'm just a man with problems! And you—are—dead!*

Get out. Please, Marcus. Just go.

I stare at my Marianne and see her screaming as the walls cave in and the floor gives out and the wires in the wall pop and fizzle, and sparks fly, and in that moment of moments—the brief second before the world caves in, she thinks of me. She thinks of me and I bring her final comfort as she feels herself falling and hitting the debris and falling falling falling—

I'll go, I whisper. *My God, I'm already gone.*

She waits by the stairs as I walk to the door.

I turn.

I love you, Marianne. I've always loved you, and I missed you after you left me.

She tears up. She starts to cry.

Please just go! she almost screams, but her heart won't let her. She still loves me. She won't hurt me by yelling. Making me feel small and childish. She's not like that. Never was. *Go, Marcus ...*

And then I'm outside, and I'm watching her close the door, and I see the door close, and I'm all alone. And Marianne is Annie. And Annie is divorced. And Annie was in her classroom. And Annie didn't die. And Annie hasn't seen me. And Annie is Annie is Annie, and is not Marianne.

And I'm alone.

And now I know it—

***

She's in the car. She's been trying to scream, but her voice won't carry. It's like a nightmare: when someone's attacking you and you try to shout but nothing comes out. Just a whisper and a breath and nothing else. She sits in the passenger's seat and watches the man—watches Ronny Feldham as he keeps glancing in the rearview mirror. And he glances at her—

Don't be scared now, he says. *I'm not gonna hurt you. I'm gonna treat you real nice. Make you feel good.*

W-what will you do?

He smiles his devil grin and his eyebrows arch and he smiles and smiles and smiles, like he knows something she doesn't. And he does. And she doesn't.

They cross Grass Street onto Bachman Avenue, coming to the house of cheese, where he slides into the driveway and gets out to open the garage. She thinks of jumping out of the car. She thinks of running off. Finding her mom and dad. Finding anyone but this man who just now eyes her in a way that makes her skin crawl.

No no no, she whispers. *No, this isn't real. This is just a dream. God give me wings. Let me fly away.*

He smiles at her and licks his lips. Walks around the truck and opens the door of the cab. *Well,* he says. *Let's get started.*

***

God give me wings so I can fly away, she thinks, eyes closed. Eyes closed real tight so the world out there will stay out there. Stay far, far away. Far away from her. She's not in the attic of the garage. He's not there. No one is there. She's alone in her special place. In her own special place where no one can get to her. Where she's the queen and no one will hurt her. Where no one can touch her. Where there's no pokepokepoke—

She waits. She waits. She waits.   She waits. She waits.

She waits. She waits. She waits. She waits. She waits.

She waits. She waits. She waits.   She waits. She waits.

She waits. She waits. She waits. She waits. She waits.

She waits. She waits. She waits. She waits. She waits.

Then he's finished. She's alone again. In the attic. Alone in the dark, and she's scared, but she's free. And the night is hers. And she's far away. Far, far, far away.

And no one can touch her.

***

I drive west on I-40. Eye for tea. Nye poor bee. Die for me. There's no one around. I'm gone. I think of my sister and feel the utter thisgrace felt because because because I letter sliphip through my fingers.

I drive down the highway and my life flashes before mice. Every last detail of my fuckedup existence. Memories. Caught in the creases on my brain. Everything a fucking memory.

And here I am.

And there you are.

And I. Am. Gone.

TWENTY: *This God Awful Demon …*

I spend my twelfth birthday at the Grand Canyon with my folks and my brother, Donald.

I walk to the edge and lean over. I haven't been well, and Mom and Dad are trying to save their marriage. Desperately. I walk to the edge and lean over, and I look down, expecting vertigo. Expecting dizziness and lightheaded euphoria. And for a moment, I think of letting go. I think of just letting go and leaning as far as I can, letting go and letting fate decide whether I live or die.

And so I do.

When Mom and Dad aren't watching, when they're busy trying to save their marriage—mostly by fighting with each other and one accusing the other—I lean and lean and lean and the whole canyon comes into view. The whole entire canyon, and for a moment's time, I *am* invincible; for a moment's time, nothing can touch me. I'm free.

Donald grabs my shoulder and throws me back onto the path we're on.

He's crying.

But that wild look in his eyes, the *Imeanbusiness* glare. The whole "big brother" façade. Too much. But I loved him for it. I loved him for trying to save me. And he was always trying to save me. And sometimes he was successful, but sometimes he failed. And although I always forgave him for failing, I don't think he did. I think on some level, he couldn't forgive himself.

That's why when I turn on the radio and I hear about the manhunt for thirty-year-old Marcus Dolby, I know that if I'm not found, he'll never recover; he'll never forgive himself. He has to protect me one last time.

I'll try and be a better older brother, he says the day I go to the hospital for the first time—with Donna and Steve and the other guys who called me faggot.

You are a good brother, I want to tell him—but don't say anything.

I love you, Marcus. You know that, right? he says as we pull into the parking lot.

I say nothing. I don't know what to say, and I hate myself for it.

He nods almost to himself.

I love you, Donald, I want to say. I have to say. I need to say. Goddamn it, say it say it say it say it!

But I say nothing. And he leaves me there. And he goes home and punishes himself in his own way. And I get better. But only for a time, and then I'll need protecting again. And I let him protect me, because I want to be protected.

***

She sits in her office and picks up the phone, but doesn't.

She sits in her office and calls her boss Martin Fairchild—but doesn't—and asks him when he wants the proposal—but doesn't—and he says to her that he's going to need it by the end of the day—but doesn't—and she tells him he'll have it by four—but doesn't—and he says, *Fine, good, thanks*—but doesn't—and she hangs up and feels so good—but doesn't—and so she takes out her laptop and is about to turn it on—but doesn't—when there is an enormous bangcrashboom from above and she looks out her window and sees debris falling to the ground—but doesn't—and the smoke that trails the debris reminds her of when she was a child and she would throw sparklers into the air on the Fourth of July, the smoke trailing the sparklesparkle—but doesn't doesn't doesn't.

None of this happened, though I think it did.

None of this happened, though I wish it did. And that's the scariest part—that I wish she was dead. That I hoped she was dead, because that would mean I'm not that crazy. That would mean that she *did* do this to me. That would mean that there's nothing really all that wrong with me. That would mean I'm going to be okay. That would mean that I won't spend the rest of my life fighting. Fighting until I'm exhausted. Fighting until I can barely stand. Fighting myself—Me with a capital *M*. Me and no one else. Fighting no one but the demon in my mind. Fighting the Voice that tells me to down Bayer, or jump out a window, or cut my motherfucking throat.

This God awful demon that has destroyed me.

***

I think of my father in one brief moment.

My father holding my hand as we walk into Fenway Park. The grass is green. Yes! The greengreen grass seems to glow and the whole park radiates from within. The conversations bleeding into a great haze of discourse. A symphony of noise. And we sit down on the third base line and my dad quickly explains to me the importance of the Sox beating the Yankees. That it's essential. That it's essential to the evolution of humankind. That the Yankees have stood in the way of human development long enough, that the Yankees retard the growth of human evolution.

As he teaches me the love and hate of baseball, I look up at him and see his features. I see his face, I watch the way his mouth—his lower lip—moves, but his upper lip is stationary. I watch his eyes as they wobble in their sockets. I watch his cheeks jostle, his eyes vibrate, his nose twitch. All of this melding together to make my dad's face *his* face, the face I remember when people ask me to describe my father.

My father was a kind and passionate man, is usually my response. But what I want to say is, *My father was a nose twitcher—you know the type—he was a cheek jostler, he was an eye wobbler—you know the type, right?* What I want to say is, *My father is every person you've ever met—and he's all mine. My dad is everything and everyone, and I'll never have another father, and I'll never have another friend like I had in my dad.*

***

I think of my dad.

I think of the three defining moments of my life in regard to my father.

I think of that day at Fenway, the hotdogs and soda pop and my dad wishing he'd brought a baseball glove for me, that he's sorry he didn't bring one, and do I mind?

No, I want to say. *No, I don't mind.*

He sits down and looks at me. *Now, Marcus, you have to understand that I don't hate George Steinbrenner professionally—you can't, he's a great businessman. No, I hate him personally. I hate him as a human being—*

And I think of the day he takes me driving for the first time when I'm fifteen, before I became bad enough to warrant me not driving until I'm seventeen. And I tell him that I'm in love Mary Ann, and—Yes! Oh my God, yes!—and he says to me, he says, *Didn't she move away—*

241

he says—*didn't she move away with her parents once her father took that teaching post down in Albuquerque?*

And I'm speechless—right now—now because I do recall that. Yes. I do recall that she did move when I was fifteen. Yes!

And then I remember the night he told me he was leaving. He comes into my room and sits down on my bed. I'm all of thirteen, and he sits down and sighs.

I need to talk to you, he says. This is the autumn after we went to the Grand Canyon. *I need to tell you something Marcus,* he says.

What's up? I ask.

I'm going to be living somewhere else, Marcus.

My jaw goes slack. My mouth drops open.

Why? Where are you going? (Can you take me, too?)

I'll be moving down near the college. It'll be easier for everyone if—

It won't be easier for me! I want to say, but don't. *It's going to fucking suck for me—what about me?* I want to say, but don't. *Please, please don't go! Please don't go, Dad. Please, just stay, you don't even have to talk to Mom! You can ignore her, but just don't leave me here!* I want to say, but don't.

I say, *Oh.*

That's it. *Oh,* I say and watch as he pats me on the head, stands up, and walks out. Four days later, he's in a house down by the college where he teaches and he's almost moved in completely a week later, with furniture from IKEA and a new Volvo. He wears clothes that his students wear, and he'll eventually marry a former student of his who dropped out and started a high-priced salon—she'll die when I'm twenty-two and Dad will be destroyed, and he'll never be with anyone else again. He'll die a little inside because he'll realize he still loves Mom, and that this woman—this former student—was his own, private version of the *mom* Dexter took away.

***

I promise my father in this moment, sitting, driving, thinking, I promise that I'll never forgive Dexter for as long as I live. No matter how chummy and nice he tries to be. I promise my dad that I'll never forgive the Rat Bastard Dex for tearing us all apart. Never.

***

She watches the moon at night for three nights. Every day she waits for his car to leave in the morning to go to the Fucking Lutheran church. He directs the choir there. He's a thin man with a gaunt face and spindly arms.

She hates him. She hates his head and his hair and his stupid fucking face. She waits in the upstairs of the garage and just sits all day, rocking back and forth on her haunches, waiting for him to come home so she can get it over with and she can stare at the moon. The moon is her friend now. She sees him—the moon—all alone up there, and she loves the moon in that instant.

She imagines being saved.

She imagines someone coming to rescue her. But that doesn't happen for four days, when she hears a commotion down in the garage and thinks it's Ronny Feldham, but then she hears many voices. She tries to shout. She tries to scream. She tries to yell.

Nothing comes out.

Like a dream. Where you run but you don't move. You shout but it's all air.

So she starts banging things around upstairs. She start throwing things around—coffee tins, fishing tackle, old dishes, glasses, boxes, books—she throws and throws with all her heart and soul until she hears a banging on the attic door—and she finally screams—*Don't go! I'm here! Please!*—and the door breaks open and up pops the head of Dexter Manning, a detective with the Glenview PD, the bastard who replaced my dad. She sees Dexter and she runs to him and he falls into her and holds her and rocks her and says, *It's okay. I got you. Shhhh. It's all okay now, but it's not okay* and she knows it as well as anyone.

But Dad didn't save her. Dexter saved her. Then he was a hero. Mom's hero. Mom's lover. Then Mom's husband, breaking my dad's heart into so many shards he never recovered. And nineteen years and two strokes later, Dexter is still married to my mom, and my brother's children call him poppy and he's family and he calls me "kid" and treats me like I'm his boy when I'm not his boy nor will I ever be and I fucking hate him and I hucking fate him he ate immediately after I kill the sonuvabitch hatehimhatehimhatehim—

Fuck you, Dex! Fuck you fuck you fuck you!

Ronny Feldham died in prison. Raped by big, burly men, no doubt.

***

Grand Canyon: eighty-nine miles. Eighty-nine matey mine Katie spine the sign says.

I drive Pinto Arizona and seea sign on the road. Turn the radio off. AM radio was nonstop news breaks asking people to call a number if they see a silver BMW with license plate number—

Please call the New Mexico State Police if you have any information regarding the whereabouts of Mister Marcus Dolby …

TWENTY-ONE: *A Hazy Realness to the Inevitable ...*

I drive west on I-40. There's no one around. I'm gone—

Wait—

I can hear talk in the background. They're trying to find me. Get me. Put me in the hospital again with Wart and Jail Bait and Beefy Guy and shit on the floor and small juice cups and Kafka Kafka Kafka!—

No, no, no!

Yes!—

Oh, I don't know. It's just that you never mentioned a Marianne until this past summer, and when you told me about her, you said you'd met at a library. And why didn't you tell me she was pregnant? I would think you'd want to confide something of that magnitude with someone—

I look around for a sign.

Wait a m—

Mem-mem-or-mory—

Yesyesyesnoyes—

Like the corners of my mind—

In Louisville, I veer off the road and find myself on I-64 driving west and I don't give a shit either way. I'm so fucking pissed off. I'm angry at God Ken Mom Dad Suzanne Donald Marianne Ted Bailey Jesus-Fucking-Christ himself! I don't give a good goddamn! What the fuck is this? Why me? Why the *fuck*—

No—yes!

I mean—

Okay. Calm. Relax.

Wait—

***

I don't feel anything but the bumps on the road below me. I feel a hazy realness to the inevitable. Everything floats by me and I'm filled with piteous thoughts. There's nothing. There is absolutely nothing right now.

Just me and my brain.

When did this all start?

Pinpoint it …

Well, I guess my last real memory was—

What?

I close my eyes and drive. I let fate decide if I live or if I die.

And I just don't care.

I simply do not care. If I live, then what? If I die, whatever. I just don't give a good God damn one way or the other.

This is where my life has taken me. This is where I end up. This is it. I have nothing. There is nothing. Marianne. Suzanne. Marianne. Suzanne. Marianne Suzanne Marianne Suzanne Marianne Suzanne Marian neSuzanneMarianneSuzanne—Annie Annie Annie.

What now?

What the fuck do I do now?

***

I feel absolutely numb. Don't feel. Nothing. Not high, not low. I feel ...pale. Road swoops under me. Lines in the center meld together. Form one solid yellow blipblipblip in front of me. Someone is kneading my brain. There's a coin in the center of my head and someone's trying to dig it out—

No. No no no nonononononono—

Hold on—

Yes! Remember. What Donald?

Yes—

My skin crawls as I sit in the pen. The pile of a state trooper stands over the desk to my right, badmouthing me to his supervisor. The clerk across from him keeps glancing over at me and nodding. Not knowing what the hell is going on is the biggest frustration of all. The officer walks past my cell and shakes his head—

Now you listen, you fucking freaky fuck, he says, walking towards me. *You come into my office, and you ream me out? Fuck no! I'll tell you something. The reason no one likes you is because you're a fucking drag, man. You make everyone feel shitty. You're a fucking downer! You want to know the truth? I have no fucking clue who this Marianne is—*

The car starts and Donald comes between Mom and Dexter. He's holding Maxine, my niece. She waves goodbye to her crazy uncle. And then Leigh walks out the door with a plate of cookies or brownies or somesuch, and runs over to Donald's car, gives me a kiss on the forehead and hands me what turns out to be pumpkin bars—

No—

Yes—no!

***

Cactus—

Brush—

Horny Toad—

Snake—

Rock—

Snake—

Honey Toad—

Brush—

Cactus—

The world on a continuous loop. Watch as it passes me by. Don't move. Don't move or I'll shoot. I told you I would. But you didn't believe me. Bang! Bang bang you're dead putabullet in yourhead. I stay stationary. Am motionless. I am a planet unto myself. I am the end all be all. I am a rock. I am an island.

There is no one around. If I turn right, I reach it— I reach the Grand Canyon. Highway 180. It seems to radiate.

***

When you get bad—and I mean, really bad, *you'll get what in layman's terms are "cyclical thoughts." It's severe psychosis. Your mind is so confused that it turns in circles. Say you're severely psychotic—something has triggered a psychotic reaction, something traumatic or whatever—you'll begin having cyclical thoughts—*

I see Beefy Guy step out of the employee bathroom with a big, satisfied smile on his face, relief washed over him; it looked like he just had the best orgasm of his life. Then Jail Bait stepped out, looking hurt and degraded—

251

I wake up at eight in the morning thinking I'm at home in bed with Marianne next to me. Turning over I smile big and say hello to my goddamn pillow. She's dead. I keep forgetting. It's amazing what the mind chooses to forget—

I eat breakfast and swallow down my yellow fluff (eggs) and leather straps (bacon), swill down the Sunny Delight and try to finish the coffee they gave me that so obviously came from an AA meeting down the street—

Wait wait wait—

No—

Not there—

I was not allowed to smoke. I was not allowed to read. I was not allowed to eat anything but the hospitalapproved menu. I was not allowed to watch TV unless it was watched during the designated "TV time," every night at 8:00. I was not allowed to open windows, wear belts, wear shoelaces, use sharp silverware, shave, go near curtains, listen to music (except at dance therapy, of course), go near female patients unless we were in group meetings (big fucking loss). I couldn't use the phone unless I cleared it with an assistant or an orderly. I couldn't have visitors and I couldn't write letters—

No!

I have others—

Please—

No!—

***

Highway 180 merges with some other road-toad. And who the fuckuckucktruck cares? I'm running out of timelimechimedime, and I want to see it before I go-go-oh. Before I go before I go before I go.

The radio says they'll find me today. Goodgoodgood. It's about fucking time, Donald!

Mile after milemilemile and I get closer and clo-loser.

Now where?

Oh, right—

Yes!—

I stop the car. I'm at the sideside-ofthe-sideahda of the roadroad. And it coco-occurs to me that I may be in trouble here. I may be in trouble here. I may be in trouble here. I may be in trouble.

There's something coming in my rearview. Miles down the ro-doad there is a cloud of dust. Vague lights.

My head's-mind-dime's playing tricks on me!

Yes!

What did he say? What did he say to me?

Sometimes memories keep you sane, Donald says to me. So I'll find them. *Memories help you remember the bad so you'll know the good,* he says. *Memories help you remember the good so you'll get through the bad,* he says.

Please think-kink-ink-nk!

Pleasepleaseplease!

You don't have much time!

Yes! Wait!

No!

Okay.

Calm. Relax. Focus—

Thankfully, Pewterschmidt was there and he said he'd get me home. We left and I told him that I was feeling under the weather and I needed sleep. He asked if I wanted to go to his place and sleep there, that there was a pullout bed and I could rest. I said I'd be fine. He insisted on taking me to my place, so we got on a Brooklynbound R and sat in silence until we passed Whitehall Street. Under the East River, he told me that people at work were talking—

No—

Faster!

***

The sin is sutting. I can see behind me. Yesyes. I can see them now. But that's all I see. Them. Coming. For me.

And I'm scared. Desert hospital. Donald, come—comequick.

***

Memories. Memories. Memories. Memories. Memories. Memories. Memories. Memories. Memories. Memories. Memories. Memories. Memories. Memories. Memories.

***

Please, dear God!

Give me—

Ken breaks off from the crowd and strides over to me.

You think this is over?

I say nothing. I want to say something—*anything! Christ!*—but nothing comes out. It's so frustrating to want to say something so badly and to have nothing come to mind—

No.

Wait.

Fasterfasterfaster—

Well, I guess my first real memory was—

Well, I guess my last real memory was—

Okay—

You—you must—yes!

Goodgood!

Tell them! Tell them what your—

Tell them all!

They're—

Yes! Tell them—

***

The air around the office is dense with confusion and fear and incomprehension. No one here will ever know what it's like to lose control. No one here knows what it's like to be afraid of yourself. No one here understands my fear and madness—

No—

No! Please no!

I guess my first memory was—

Wait, wait, wait …

My last memory was—

No, no … wait.

Okay. Calm. Relaxed. Think now.

Now try, try, try.

Do it!

Memories of my existence caught in the creases of my brain: Mother holding, Father leaving, teacher yelling, everything just a memory. Memory with a capital *M*. So, so, so, what do I recall? What do I know is real? Tell me tell me tell me, because I have to know! You've got to do this, just once! Write them, shout them, think them, but dear God, hurry! Dear God, make it quick because there's not much time now!—

No—

Memories, memories, memories. *Sometimes memories keep you sane,* says Donald.

Yes!

Wait.

I'm in my living room and I get a call from Marianne, my girlfriend, and she tells me that something just ran into her building. (Some asshole flew a fucking plane into her building downtown.) Later I turn on channel four. Horror. I watch the tape as another jet runs into the other tower, and about an hour or two later, they both fall over with her and thousands of other people inside as well.

Wait.

The knife seems to glide across my skin. Nothing. It would be nice to feel something. *Anything!* I feel the blood dribble down my neck, the evil wetness of it seeping into my shirt collar. My mind bubbles to life with the realization that I'm about to die! This is it! I cut deeper! Deeper! Yes! I'm gonna die! Wait, wait, wait, wait, wait, wait, wait …

Wait—

I guess my last real—

Wait.

No. Wait.

I guess. I guess my last—wait! I guess my last memory was—I guess I guess—

...I guess my last real, lucid, vivid memory was of my widowed mother crying—weeping—as she watched my roommate Bailey take a shit on the floor in the mental ward of St. Michael the Hope...

Wait ...

PLEASE, STOP READING!

Please don't read this …

Pleasepleaseplease, I beg you this one favor. Stop reading this. Please! I mean it, don't continue, because the story does end where it began. That was the ending, in all actuality. In all honesty. No shit.

The thoughts that keep cycling like the fucking Tour de France—going and going and going—and they never stop. So don't expect this to be a happy ending, because it isn't happy. There really are no happy endings anymore. There's always something fucking up the cogs, getting the gears all shifty and loose. So don't read any further. There's no story after the car, after the desert, the Grand Canyon. There's no brother Donald running to the car, there's no Donald screaming for the medics, the police aren't running around like chickens sans heads, and I'm not mumbling incoherently—

… I guess my last real, lucid, vivid memory was of my widowed mother crying—weeping—as she watched my roommate Bailey take a shit on the floor in the mental ward of St. Michael the Hope …

Wait.

Printed in the United States
122836LV00001B/103-126/P